LEVON'S HUNT

A VIGILANTE JUSTICE THRILLER
BOOK 9

CHUCK DIXON

ROUGH EDGES PRESS

Levon's Hunt
Paperback Edition
© Copyright 2022 (As Revised) Chuck Dixon

Rough Edges Press
An Imprint of Wolfpack Publishing
1707 E. Diana Street
Tampa, FL 33610

roughedgespress.com

This book is a work of fiction. References to historical events, real people, or real places are used fictitiously. Any similarity to real persons, living or dead, is purely coincidental and not intended by the author.

All brand names and product names used in this book are trademarks, registered trademarks, or trade names of their respective holders. Wolfpack Publishing is not associated with any product or vendor in this book.

Paperback ISBN 978-1-68549-044-7
eBook ISBN 978-1-68549-034-8

LEVON'S HUNT

LEVON'S HUNT

The wash of rainwater on the windshield transformed the motel front into a sprawling palace of lights against the gloom of night. The neon that spelled out Cedar Creek Motor Lodge turned the wet parking lot into a galaxy of primary colors; constellations appeared and disappeared when the letters winked on and off.

Lex Krogstad gripped the wheel of his Sonata and blinked through the frigid spray coming in through his open window. He found Room Eleven easily enough. It was the only one with a vehicle parked in front of it. A pickup truck gleamed beetle-slick in the steady downpour. The truck was backed into the spot before number eleven. Lex spun the wheel to guide his car into the spot next to the truck with his rear bumper facing the building to conceal his license plate.

The door was answered by a man a good head taller than Lex, a broad-shouldered bastard in a work shirt and jeans, a leather pouch for a clasp knife on his tooled belt. Lex looked down to see this guy wore yellow leather work boots. Some kind of redneck.

"You Tilitser?" The man's smile did not reach as far as his eyes.

The drawl made Lex change his mind. Not a redneck. A hillbilly.

"That makes you Whistler seven three," Lex said.

"Come on in," the big man said and stepped back into the room. A double with two full-size beds, still made up except for the indent where the man had been lying, watching the room's ancient analog television. The walls were covered in ersatz paneling with a fading print of imitation wood grain. A sofa painting hung over each bed. One was of sunflowers, and the other featured a thatch-roofed hovel in an idyllic glen.

"Where's our friend?" Lex asked as he closed the door behind him.

"In the shower," the big man said, slouching back on pillows stacked against the headboard. One foot up on the bed, the other resting on the floor.

"Oh, yeah?" The door to the bathroom was closed. He could hear the running water over the downpour drumming on the roof and windows.

"He's a little nervous. Wants to make sure he's all cleaned up for you."

"Okay."

Lex looked at the TV, which was playing at low volume. Some old black and white show with a pair of lawyers arguing in a courtroom. His mom used to love those kinds of shows.

"You brought the money, right?" the big man said.

"Yes. Yes." Lex dug into the interior pocket of his damp windbreaker and pulled out an envelope sealed with tape.

The big man made a gimme gesture and Lex tossed him the packet. The man tore it open, plucked out the contents, and quickly riffled the bills. It was the amount they had agreed on. The man nodded and hiked a hip off the bed to jam the folded stack of fifties into the front pocket of his jeans. Lex took a seat on the edge of a chair next to the room's pressed-wood dresser.

The meet had been set up on a website that Lex visited frequently: quellefromage.net. He posted there as Tillister, while the man on the bed used the screen name Whistler73. It was an old-school chat room that, to the eye of anyone casually stumbling upon it, appeared to deal with the subject of gourmet cheese. Any actual cheese fanciers attempting to make sense of it would find the posts confusing. There were many postings about ages, weights, and imports of certain cheeses but few specifics about texture, flavor, or sharpness.

Any sincere posts about cheese were simply ignored in favor of longer threads that seemed to represent the negotiations for private sales. Most of those offerings were for quite unusual amounts of cheese at often steep prices. Even the most ardent foodie was not about to pay one thousand dollars for thirty-two pounds of five-year-old Dorblu.

"Um, I didn't ask on the site," Lex said, breaking the awkward silence. "But what sort of boy is he?"

"What sort?" The man on the bed's disinterested gaze remained on the TV.

"Is he a white boy? Or colored?"

"That matter? If it matters, you needed to say something." The man turned to him.

"No. Not really. They're all pink on the inside, aren't they?" Lex gave a simpering laugh at his own remark.

The man's faux smile returned; the eyes remained flinty.

"He's a colored boy. Light skin. His name is Lester," the man said. "Why don't you go on and take a look?"

"You think that'd be okay?"

"Sure. Go on ahead." The man waved a hand toward the bathroom. "I'll just let myself out and leave the two of you alone."

"If you think it would be okay." Lex half-rose from the chair.

"You paid your money, friend." The man sat on the edge of the mattress to retie the lace of one of his boots.

Lex's heart was pounding as he crossed the room to the bathroom door. His face was flushed, and he felt an excitement building. A trickle of sweat rolled down the nape of his neck and the room suddenly felt warm. His hand touched the knob, and he eased the door open. The patter of water from the showerhead grew louder. He stepped onto the damp tile. The tub was enclosed by an avocado-green shower curtain streaked rusty with mold. The room was fuggy with damp air, the mirror over the sink fogged.

"Lester?" Lex's voice came out a croak, his throat constricted with anticipation.

There was no answer, only the uninterrupted hiss of the shower water.

"You can call me Uncle Lex." He reached for the edge of the curtain and drew it back.

Cold water streamed from the showerhead into an empty tub.

Something like lightning flashed behind Lex's eyes. An intense burning sensation started at the base of his neck to lance through every extremity and turned his legs numb. A second bolt of lightning struck him in the small of the back. His legs folded beneath him. His last memory was of the cracked porcelain edge of the cast-iron tub rushing up to meet his fall.

2

He woke shivering.

A dull ache in his head built to a hammering pain that rose and fell with each heartbeat. He opened his eyes, and the pain rose a notch in the bright light reflected off the white tile.

Lex Krogstad was buck-naked in a tub filled with cold water, the same tub in which he'd expected to find the six-year-old "Cheshire" he'd paid five hundred dollars for. More than naked, wet, and alone, he found that his wrists were bound behind him with what felt like plastic straps. A strip of tape covered his mouth, the glue bitter when he explored it with his tongue. He tried to call out, then to scream. It was barely audible against the torrential downpour hammering the roof in a near-empty motel far from the highway outside a flyspeck Georgia town the week after Christmas.

The water had a pink tinge to it. He looked down to see streaks of his own blood on his chest. It was dripping from the end of his nose. The blow on the tub's edge must have split the skin. It sure hurt like the devil.

The door opened, and the big man in the work boots

entered. He now wore a canvas farmer's coat and a pair of blue vinyl gloves. Lex was more concerned with what the man carried in each arm.

Two twenty-pound plastic bags of ice like the kind you buy out front of a Speedway or 7-Eleven.

The pain in his head forgotten, Lex mewled through the tape over his mouth. The man rested the bags on the toilet lid to slice the tops open with a clasp knife. Lex's mewling turned to an animal keening when the man upended the bags of ice and dumped them into the tub. Displaced water rose over the lip to spread across the tile floor.

He bucked and squirmed as ice mounded on his crotch. The cubes burned with a cold fire against his genitals. He looked pleadingly at his tormentor, muffled squeaks escaping through the slab of duct tape plastered across his mouth.

The man took a seat on the lid of the toilet and fished a smartphone from the pocket of his coat.

"I'm going to ask you some questions now," the man said.

Lex nodded, bobbing his head, ready to say anything to get out of the icy bath that was already turning his hands and feet blue.

"And I need you to be honest with me." The man touched the phone screen. "Don't be lying, thinking I'm going to believe just anything and let you out of that tub."

Lex's nodded assent grew more emphatic. His entire body was shuddering with the cold.

"Take a look at this here." The man held the phone out for him to see.

He fought down his tremors to focus on the video playing on the phone. It was of poor quality, but the setting was well lit, and the subjects were in plain view.

There were two people in the shot: a white man with a skein of tattoos covering his upper arms and back and a boy, a dark boy, Mexican maybe, of about eight or nine. Both were naked and in a bedroom of some kind, a residence rather than a motel.

Normally, this was the sort of video Lex might have enjoyed. He had thousands of hours of this same kind of stuff stored on an external hard drive at his house in Augusta. The only sensation he felt viewing *this* video was the clutch of the icy water. His manhood, such as it was, had retreated into his groin in a vain attempt to escape the freezing grip.

"You know this man?" the man in the work boots asked.

"I-I-I-I can only see his back." Lex fought down convulsions to speak clearly.

The man touched a finger to the screen to advance the video and held it before Lex's face again.

"You know him?"

The man in the video lay on his back, the boy atop him. The man's face was clear now. Lex recognized him. The video was from a few years before, maybe ten or more, but it was unmistakably a man he'd met a time or two.

"You do know him." The man took the phone back.

Lex nodded, the motion uncontrollable as the shakes wracked his body. His teeth were chattering hard, his jaw muscles bunched with the effort. He never knew cold could be this painful.

"Tell me his name."

Any idea of either withholding the name or making one up fled from Lex's mind. His only desire was to get out of this tub, to escape the numbing cold before his heart failed or he passed out and drowned in his own filth. He blurted the name, even spelling it, enunciating each letter through lips now torn and bloody, ripped by his chattering teeth.

The man entered the name on his phone, taking care, his big, callused index finger unaccustomed to such delicate work.

"Y-y-y-y-y-you got what you want," Lex stammered

The man rose and left the room.

"I-I-I-I-I gave you the name!" he shouted, his voice bouncing off the tiled walls. "N-n-n-n-now you let me go!"

The man returned with two more bags of ice and sliced them open.

Lex shrieked, his voice hoarse even as he felt his breathing begin to slow. "W-w-w-w-w-w-we made a deal! I-I-I-I-I-I gave you the name!"

"I never made any promises," Levon Cade said.

He upended the bags to fill the tub to the brim once more.

3

"Looks like a plain and simple heart attack to me," the EMT said.

"Bullshit," the EMT's female partner said. It came out, "boo-*shit*."

The EMTs finished strapping the sheet-covered corpse on the gurney. Water dripped off it and into the matted carpet of the motel room. They'd found the man in the tub, as pale as the sheet that covered him.

"What's she talking about, Hank?" Sheriff Dane Willets asked the man, Henry Fellowes. Henry was a young man Dane knew from playing Pop Warner ball with one of his sons.

One of his deputies, the first responder, stood looking idly about the room. Good kid, Bob Coates, in his third year out of Forsyth. This was Dane's first term as sheriff of Pickens County after twenty years of driving a prowl car, and he was only the second black man to hold that post. He relied on men like Coates to help him keep that position.

Bristling at being referred to in the third person, the

sister said, "I'm talking about how he was head-to-toe *blue*, Sheriff."

"You're saying it wasn't his heart?" Dane asked.

"Mighta been," she said. She and Hank hauled the gurney up and locked it upright. "But it was caused by hypothermia."

"You mean he froze to death?"

"Looks that way to me," she said.

The EMTs rolled the gurney out into the late morning light.

"Froze to death in a motel bathtub," Dane said. He watched them load the gurney into the back of the ambulance. "What're y'all, *Quincy* now?"

Both EMTs, who were in their twenties, stared blankly at him.

"You run a tox screen on this guy," Hank said. "Hunnerd to one it's the oxy."

"Naw. Naw." The sister shook her head. "I pulled a kid outta Little Pine last winter. Looked just like this man here. All blue and shit. And not exposure neither. Hypothermia."

"It wasn't that cold last night," Dane said.

"All's I'm sayin' is what I'm sayin'," the sister said with a shrug. Her partner sealed the back of the van.

They climbed into the cab and rolled off the lot. Dane rejoined his deputy inside. Bob Coates had the contents of the man's wallet laid out on the bed. He was going through the cards and inserts with gloved hands.

"So, who was he?"

Bob read from the driver's license: "Alexander Davies Krogstad. Up here from Peachtree. That's his car out front. He's a schoolteacher, according to his union card. And, huh, still has a Blockbuster membership. Thought all those places was closed."

"Well, there's a clue. The man was a procrastinator at cleaning out his wallet."

"You think she was right, Sheriff? Think this fella froze to death?"

"I don't know what to think. Man checks into a motel alone, less than a day's ride from his home, to take a bath and wakes up dead."

"You want me to tape the room off?"

"Naw, Bob. Just lock her up when we leave. I'll ask the manager not to rent her out until further notice. Won't be much of a sacrifice this time of year. Most all these rooms are empty anyhow."

Dane made for the door and turned before leaving.

"Bob, you know who Quincy is?" he said.

"That's one of the Muppets, right?" the deputy replied.

———

THE FIRST THING Dane did upon arriving at the office was to fire off an email to the county coroner requesting a toxicology screen on Alexander Krogstad. It was more out of idle curiosity than any suspicion of foul play. It might only be an overdose like Hank said, and maybe the guy just had poor circulation. Still, he knew if he didn't have it confirmed one way or the other, it would gnaw at him.

He next called the high school in Peachtree where the deceased worked and was not surprised to find it was still closed for the holidays. Bob Coates brought him Krogstad's wallet in an evidence bag. He pulled on gloves and went through the contents. From the three-digit number following his street address, Krogstad lived in an apartment building. It took a call to the police office in Peachtree to learn that the address was an apartment complex called Westchase Heights. The building manager informed Dane that Mr. Krogstad lived alone, was divorced, and his wife lived in Florida with her new husband. They had no children, and as far as the manager knew, had no relatives that ever visited him, though he'd ask among the other tenants.

Just after lunch, Dane's secretary came on the intercom to announce he had a call from the GBI on Line One.

"Special Agent Cy Godshall, Sheriff," a husky smoker's voice said on the speakerphone. "I understand you have an Alexander Krogstad DOA in your morgue. His name rang a few bells here."

"Well, he's over to the funeral home here in Jasper," Dane said. "That's where our coroner does his work."

"Could I ask you to put a hold on any further investigation until I have time to get down there?"

"Well, the fella ain't going nowhere. Turns out he didn't have much in the way of family. When were you thinking of getting here?"

"I'll be there before five, barring traffic."

"Well, I'll be here whenever you get here, Agent Godshall," Dane said. He made a mental note to call home and tell his wife he might be late for supper.

———

THE GBI AGENT arrived closer to six, apologizing and cursing the traffic. He was a big, bluff man with a red nose whose overcoat smelled of nicotine just as Dane suspected it might. He had in tow a second agent, a blonde girl with a turned-up nose and the build of a runner. He introduced her as Special Agent Lindsay Dauber.

"Never thought I'd live to see the roads clogged like

this," Godshall said as he shook Dane's hand. "Fast as we build new highways, they fill 'em up."

"Has to be all the Yankees movin' down this way," Dane said, smiling.

"You have a problem with Yankees, sheriff?" Agent Dauber said without a trace of a drawl.

"Notice I didn't say *damn* Yankees," Dane said, bringing out a rumbling chortle from Agent Godshall.

The agents used their unmarked car to follow Dane in his county car to Royal's Funeral Home. He'd called ahead to ask Billy Royal to stay and wait for his guests from Decatur. They entered the funeral home through the service entrance that led to an extensive basement complex and the morgue.

Alexander Krogstad lay naked and supine on the embalming table. A plastic band with his DOD, full name, and a bar code was affixed around his right wrist.

"I took fluid for the tox screen as you asked, Sheriff," Billy said. "Otherwise, I've not touched him." Billy was the oldest member of the Royal clan still working in the mortuary business since his father retired ten years earlier. The family had been preparing folks for burial since before the Confederacy.

"Any guess as to time of death?" Agent Dauber asked.

"Hard to say. His body temperature was very low when we took it. I understand he was found in a tub of water."

"He wasn't checked into the motel, but the night manager says his car wasn't there before ten last night," Dane added.

"Has to have died within the last eighteen hours then," Agent Godshall said.

"Not with that core body temperature," Billy said as he shook a Pall Mall from a pack.

"Mind if I smoke?" Godshall asked and pulled a crumpled box and lighter from his coat pocket.

"I don't mind. I mostly just let mine burn. Covers the more unpleasant odors." Billy accepted a light from the GBI man.

"What do you mean about his temperature, sir?" Agent Dauber said.

"This man's core temp was at the level of a man dead much longer than last night. I'd put it twenty-four hours or more before the time he was brought in here."

"That's not possible unless a dead man drove to that motel last night," Dauber said.

"Or someone drove him there in his own car," Godshall said.

"Or he froze to death," Dane said.

Everyone turned to him.

———

IT WAS DETERMINED from various tests that Alexander Krogstad had indeed frozen to death.

Or rather, his heart had seized after prolonged exposure to cold, bringing on hypothermia. How this was accomplished was pure speculation. His toxicology screen came back negative for drugs, alcohol, or any toxins, though he did experience a severe blow to the head that was forceful enough to split the skin at the hairline, bruise the frontal lobe of the brain, and cause a mild concussion. The autopsy also revealed two pairs of burn marks, one pair to the nape of the neck and another set to the lower back. Then there was the matter of the livid bruises around the wrists of both hands.

Someone had tied him up.

"I can think of worse ways to go," Agent Godshall

said. He stirred his third refill of coffee at the Waffle House on 53. "You just drift off to sleep."

"Not like any homicide I've ever seen," Dane said and spooned up some Bert's Chili. It was close to ten and long past suppertime with the family. "Why kill a man that way?"

"More like torture gone wrong." Agent Dauber poked her fork at what passed for a salad at the Waffle House. "They hit him twice with a stun gun. I'm betting that's how he got the head injury. Whanged his forehead on the tub surround or sink edge when he fell."

"So, what did they want? Did they *get* what they wanted?" Godshall asked. "Either way, we make this a crime scene. We'll be taking this bugger off your hands, Sheriff."

"That suits me fine, Agents. But if you can tell me, what's the state bureau's interest in a dead schoolteacher?"

"He was a bad boy, Sheriff," Godshall said.

"A *very* bad boy," Dauber put in.

4

The early morning air was crisp and clean closer to the top of the ridge. The sun had not risen high enough to burn off the thick fog that filled the holler below like soup in a bowl. An overnight dusting of snow would make the two-toed marks of deer stand out as clear as words on a page. Levon Cade stood with his daughter Merry on the lee side of the trunk of a tall pine and watched the dawn light spill across the top of the clouds of mist like butter melting on a pile of mashed potatoes.

"How long you think we need to wait?" Merry said, adjusting her mittened grip on the stock of the Hawken rifle.

"Till this fog clears," Levon said. "You aren't getting impatient, are you?"

"Just cold. This wind coming over the ridge is making my butt numb."

"Can't go down in the holler till we can see our way and other folks can see us."

"You think there's other hunters down there?"

"Could be. You never know. But till there's a clear line of sight, we stay right here."

Levon crouched by her, his .54 caliber rifle across his knees. As they watched, the tops of the fog bank turned to wisps of rising vapor cut through by rays of the light coming over the far hill.

"You think this is okay?" Merry asked, breaking a long silence.

"What's okay, honey?"

"You taking me hunting like this?"

"Don't other dads take their kids out for deer?"

"Sure. If they're *boys*. Dads take their sons."

"You wanted to come along someday. You've been asking since you could talk."

"I wanted to go Disneyworld someday, too."

"I promise I'll get you there, Merryberry."

"I know you will, Dad." She turned to him, her freckled nose wrinkling above the smile hidden by the woolen scarf wrapped around her face.

"Hope, too," Levon said in reference to Merry's adopted sister.

"You might have to *keep* your promise to Hope. She's got no interest in hunting."

"Well, I suppose it's not in her blood. It's in yours, though. Cades have been hunting these hills a long time."

"With rifles like these?" Merry patted the burnished tiger-striped stock of the heavy percussion rifle.

"Much like these. Only I doubt any Cade ever had weapons as fine as this." Levon had built the two muzzle-loaders over the summer from kits purchased on Hawken's website. He and Merry had practiced loading and firing and zeroed them on the range in back of Uncle Fern's farm.

They were quiet for a while longer, watching the sky turn pink to the east and the fog drift clear of first the pine tops and then the boles of the trees below. It clung to the boughs like cotton before the wind rising up the incline began to stir it and spread it, and finally caused it to vanish.

"Dad?"

"Yes, honey?"

"Do you wish you had a son instead of a daughter?"

He turned to her. She kept her gaze steady toward the holler floor.

"You've never said anything like that before."

"This is our first time hunting. I was only wondering if this was something you'd rather be doing with a son."

Levon touched the shoulder of her quilted coat with his gloved fingers. She turned her head to look at him.

"Honey, there's nobody in this whole world I'd rather be here with right now than you."

Her nose crinkled in answer.

"Now, let's get us a buck so your uncle can stop complaining his chest freezer is empty," Levon said.

Side by side, they walked down the incline, rifles cradled in their arms.

———

A NARROW STREAM ran along the floor of the holler, narrow enough to cross in a leap.

There was a confusion of prints in the snow along both banks where a game trail crossed the iced-over water. The daintier tracks of varmints such as possums and raccoons mixed with the impressions left by deer. Some larger animal had pawed a hole through the inch-thick ice to reveal the water trickling below on its way to the base of the five-mile-long gully.

Levon handed his binoculars to Merry, who braced herself against the bole of a birch to steady her hand.

"What do you see?" he asked, voice low.

"Looks like most of the tracks are on the far bank,"

she said, holding the lenses away from her eyes the way her father had shown her. "Like they came down the hill for a drink and went back up the same way into those black oaks."

"How long ago?"

"Since the snow stopped. The prints going back up the hill are clear."

"How many you guess there are?"

"I dunno. Five. Maybe six. It gets kind of mixed up."

"That would be my guess, too," Levon said. He rose from his crouch and scanned the trees to their right. "I say we move along south here and cross the stream where it goes into those pines."

Merry pointed at the trail below with the binoculars. "But the tracks go east."

"Once the buck leads his herd into the oaks, he's gonna hook one way or the other. Left or right. I'm guessing right."

"Why pick the right?"

"Gotta pick one. And the trail follows a shelf of land up toward the razorback."

"You can see that?" Merry raised the binoculars to squint through the lenses. She glassed the steep incline but saw nothing but beeches and pines.

"I told you, I've hunted here before. I wasn't much older than you the first time." Levon moved along the slope to the south.

Merry replaced the caps on the binoculars before hanging them around her neck. She adjusted the Hawken over her shoulder and followed her father.

The sun rose higher in the sky to touch the tops of the trees. The snow that was weighing down the higher boughs began to melt. Droplets fell through the leaves like light rain. The constant patter covered the sound of the two hunters moving through the spruce and red cedar that covered the eastern slope of the holler.

Levon reached the false crest first. He dropped down on the soft bed of pine needles to wave a hand back at Merry. A narrow ledge of rocky earth followed the wall of the holler a stone's throw shy of the ridgeline. The milky sunlight of the open sky was barely visible through the trees above them. They moved with care along the downslope below the ledge, Levon taking turkey peeks over the lip every few steps. He stopped, crouched, and turned to Merry to cock his head upslope.

Merry held her breath and listened. From somewhere above, a sound could be heard under the dripping snowmelt: a raspy bellow that rose and fell before dying away. Her father crept on his hands and knees under a low-hanging cedar bough. She followed, the spiny needles brushing the back of her coat. Ice-cold slush dripped on her exposed neck.

She kept on, duck-walking while her father moved low over the slick surface of a rocky ledge to take cover behind the massive girth of a fallen red oak. Merry dropped down beside him. The bellow was more pronounced here. Levon slipped his rifle from his shoulder and gestured for her to do the same.

They slid the rifles over the top of the deadfall and sighted down the long barrels to sweep the slope above. Merry watched for movement the way her father had taught her. The bough of a longleaf pine shuddered about fifty yards above their position. She focused her eyes past the front tang at the end of the octagonal barrel and could see in the shadows under a lowering bough a doe and two fawns nested there. The two yearlings lay with their long legs folded under them, pressed to their mother's side for warmth.

Another bellow, more of a bark. It sounded closer than before. Inch by inch, Merry shifted the barrel, looking for the source of the sound over her sights, and caught a hint of movement, a change in the light. She strained her eyes, searching for the cause.

Nearly invisible on the other side of a shaft of watery winter sunlight stood a buck, a full twelve-point bull with a barrel chest and powerful legs. His hooves were set firm in the black earth beneath the snow, ready for a leap. Mist drifted from his nostrils as he turned his antlered head from side to side. His head was not fully raised, and his ears were at rest. He had not sensed the presence of hunters.

Merry pulled the mitten from her right hand with her teeth. She wore fingerless woolen gloves beneath. She took in a long breath and letting it out slowly as she tucked the end of the stock firmly into her shoulder. She relaxed her left hand under the fore stock and allowed the heavy rifle to rest on it as she drew back the hammer with her right thumb. Another breath, another exhale, and she fixed the big animal in her sights. The front tang was set on the thickly furred neck just before the shoulder.

"He's all yours," her father said in a whisper. "Remember what I told you."

"Control my breathing. Both eyes open. Squeeze, don't pull."

With her index finger firm on the trigger, Merry pressed until she felt the tension in the pull. She blinked and refocused her eyes. The buck turned his head toward her, seeming to look her right in the eyes.

A hammer blow struck close enough to them to send a shower of bark fragments flying off the dead oak. Merry's reflexes caused her to jerk the trigger home. The fat lead ball went high on a thick cloud of yellow smoke. The thunderous roar of the Hawken filled the air.

She was pulled back by her father's grip on her collar. She heard the flat echo of an explosion from somewhere far above them. Her father dragged her flat on the snow and lay atop her to shield her.

"Someone else is hunting here?" she said in a hush.

"That shot was at us," her father said in a hoarse murmur.

"What do we do about it?"

"Nothing. I'm going to get you out of here. When I fire, run like hell back to those pines."

Her father moved ten feet or so along the length of the dead oak, staying flat to the ground the whole way.

Merry drew her legs under her in a low crouch. She watched her father crane his head sideways to scan the slope above with one eye. He laid that way for the longest minutes of her life. With a single fluid movement, he raised up on one knee and fired the muzzle-loader at something up the hill. A thick plume of sulfurous smoke enveloped him. Merry launched herself across the narrow shelf to slide under the pine boughs and out of sight.

A second report rang out on the heels of the whicketing sound of a round tearing through the branches high above.

Levon dropped alongside Merry. He lay in the concealment of the shadows and swiftly reloaded the Hawken, placing a new percussion cap in place and thumbing the hammer back.

"You expect them to chase us?" Merry said, voice shaking and not from the cold.

"No. I think they were looking to discourage us." Levon levered up a branch with the end of his barrel, eyes moving across the ground above them.

"What do we do now?" she asked.

He lowered the hammer back in place against the cap.

"We go home."

5

The forensics report that came back from the Cedar Creek Motor Lodge was worth jack shit to the GBI agents assigned to the case.

While the room, like any motel room anywhere, was well-populated with DNA samples of all kinds, useful evidence was absent. Every conceivable surface that might have been touched by the room's most recent guest had been wiped clean. All doorknobs and door edges. The faucets of both the sink and bathtub were spotless, as were the toilet flush handle and lid. The bedside table had been wiped, and the TV remote. Even the room key with its numbered plastic lanyard had been scrubbed of prints.

The murder weapon, presumably a massive quantity of ice, had simply melted and gone down the drain.

The manager on duty that night at the motel said the guy who'd checked into Room Eleven had paid cash. He swore he'd looked at the guy's driver's license but couldn't recall the name. The name scrawled on the motel's clipboard entry could have been anything, like the driver's license number. When pressed, the manager said Room Eleven had been let to an "average white guy" of "average height." Nor did he happen to notice if the guest had made frequent trips to the ice machine just outside the motel office.

Agent Godshall strongly suspected this genius had never looked up from the same game of FreeCell he was playing when the GBI agents came to question him.

Since this was the local cheaters' motel, there were no surveillance cameras on the parking lot or in the office. One amenity this fleabag could offer its guests was anonymity. That meant the ice machine theory was unprovable. Further confirmation of this was the rich tapestry of fingerprints that remained on Room Eleven's ice bucket. They sent it off to have the prints cross-checked, but the assumption was the "average white guy" had bought his ice elsewhere.

A fruitless check of local convenience stores in a five-mile radius turned up no suspects that fit even the fuzzy description of "average" making mass purchases of party ice. This despite hours and hours spent by a junior agent running through surveillance footage. The suspect had either bought the ice farther out or brought it from home.

"Somebody did the state a favor," Cy Godshall said. He was standing outside the building entrance in the rear parking lot of the Georgia Bureau of Investigation center.

Lindsay Dauber nodded. She was standing upwind, arms crossed against the biting cold of a damp Georgia winter. She'd come out to join her senior on one of his twice-daily cigarette breaks, though she did not smoke. It was the only occasion, other than when they were in the field, on which they could speak freely outside the uptight confines of the Bureau. Everyone was so damned touchy these days, scared shitless about saying something that might earn them sensitivity training hours.

"This Krogstad was a piece of shit. Could have been anyone he met who might want to end his sorry life." Godshall lit his second Marlboro of the day, hands cupped around the lighter against the wind.

"How'd he keep a job as a school teacher with his record?" Lindsay was referring to Alexander Krogstad's arrest record for solicitation and "sexual knowledge of a minor."

"I guess it's who you know. And that was a while back."

"Fifteen years. But these guys don't change even after the law puts a scare in them."

"You think he was up in Pickens sniffing around?"

"He went there to meet *someone*," Lindsay said. The wind shifted in her direction, and she moved away from the stream of tobacco smoke. "Has the week off from teaching. Decides to buy himself a Christmas gift."

"Boxing Day."

"Huh?"

"Day after Christmas. They call it Boxing Day in Canada. England too, I think."

"Well, he wasn't after anyone's box."

"I read that. He likes boys." Godshall snickered, smoke escaping through his teeth.

"Maybe he met up with a pimp, a handler. Maybe he didn't like the price. There's a fight, and—"

"And the pimp decides to deep-freeze him?"

"Yeah. That doesn't work."

They stood for a while, looking out across the yellowed grass that led down to the parking lot. Godshall smoked his Marlboro down to the filter and put the butt out on the steel side of an air handler unit. They walked toward the portico that ran across the rear of the building, anxious to return to the steamy warmth of their office.

"We have other cases. Gonna have to let this one go cold."

"Good one, Cy," Dauber said with a lazy smile.

"Did *I* say that?" Godshall asked in mock innocence, eyebrows raised.

———

THE JOKE WAS ON THEM. Three days later, Dauber picked up the phone to take a call from Washington.

"Special Agent Lindsay Dauber, Georgia Bureau of Investigation, Investigative Division, how may I help you?"

"Hey, Lindsay. This is Laura Strand with the US marshals, Missing Child Unit." The voice was friendly enough on the surface, but Dauber could sense this lady was all business. And an ugly business it was, dealing with runaways, abductees, and other damaged kids.

"How can we help you, Marshal?"

"You recently reported the homicide of a known sex offender. An Alexander Krogstad of Peachtree City, Georgia." Only people outside Georgia called Peachtree "Peachtree City." Dauber had learned that in her sixth year since moving south from Long Island.

"That's still an open case."

"I think we may be able to help each other out on that one, Agent Dauber. We believe it links to several other homicide cases in the southeast. There are a number of similarities."

"You're certainly welcome to look over what we have, Marshal. Though I gotta tell you, it's not a lot. Send me your request and authorization, and we'll send you what we have."

"Actually, I'm already en route to Decatur. Another agent and I will be there this afternoon. I was hoping we could meet and share notes. It would be a big help."

"My partner and I are on the clock until five. We'll give you all the help we can."

"I've already contacted your deputy director. He's authorized overtime for both you and Agent Godshall.

"Oh. Oh, well, then. We look forward to your arrival."

"Thank you, Agent Dauber. See you in a few." The line went dead.

"Shit fuck," Dauber said. She replaced the phone in its dock.

"You have a problem, Linds?" Godshall looked up from the monitor on his desk.

"No. *We* have a problem, Cy. Feds."

"Shit fuck," Godshall said.

6

"Damnedest thing. Damnedest thing," Uncle Fern said mostly to himself as he fussed over the stovetop.

"Daddy says they were shooting at us, whoever it was." Merry sat at the table in the kitchen of the Cade farmhouse. The grilled cheese, 'mater, and onion sandwich, one of her uncle's specialties, sat untouched before her by a bowl of Campbell's tomato soup.

"Someone tried to kill you?" Hope asked, eyes wide. She was sitting in the chair opposite her.

"Daddy says they might have been trying to scare us."

"Scare you? Like those hills belong to them or like that? Like they have a goddamned right?" Fern scooped a finished sandwich from the skillet with a spatula and dropped it on a fresh plate.

"Maybe it was an accident," Hope said, eyes still locked on her big sister, ignoring the plate of steaming gooey goodness her adoptive uncle placed before her.

"That's not what Daddy says. Whoever took the shot had the same line of sight on that buck as we did. It was *us* he was shooting at."

"I hunted the woods since me and your grandad were

boys. Up there I don't know how many times a year," Fern groused. "Ain't heard of an accident in season in I don't know how many years."

"It wasn't an accident," Merry insisted.

"Your daddy say what kind of round was fired at you?"

"He said something military."

"It was a .223," Levon said from the doorway as he entered the house. He'd finished cleaning the Hawkens muzzleloaders out in his work shed and had them cradled in his arms.

"You tell from the sound of it?" Fern said.

"And the keyhole impact in the wood of the tree we were using for cover."

Fern nodded in confirmation. He was as familiar as Levon with the sound of that particular round, having humped a Mike-Mike of his own in Hue City and the Ia Drang Valley during his two tours in Vietnam. The flat bark of the military round was as unmistakable as the wicked signature wound it made, which looked more like a knife puncture than a bullet strike.

"Damnedest thing," Fern grumbled. "More AR-15s in this county than sense."

"What do you do?" Hope asked around a mouthful of bread and cheese. She'd finally succumbed to the lure of the toasted sandwich. "Do you tell the police?"

"Now, you know we're not the types to bother with the law," Fern said from the counter, where he was assembling a sandwich for himself.

"Then what will you do?" Hope turned to Levon, who'd returned to the kitchen after hanging the rifles over the fireplace mantle.

"I don't see as there's anything we can do, Hope." Levon poured himself a mug of coffee and sat down before his own plate.

Merry knew by the set of her father's jaw that he had said that only for Hope's benefit.

————

LEVON RETURNED to his work shed after lunch, leaving the girls and his uncle to watch a movie in the living room. He had his own movies to watch, though he found them to be an unpleasant chore.

The steel-frame building sitting on a concrete pad and set back off the long gravel drive was a shed in name only. The size of a generous three-car garage and half again as deep, the building was home to a neat workbench that ran along the length of one wall, with stations for reloading ammunition and woodworking. The wall above the bench was covered in pegboard, with hand tools hanging from rows of hooks and pegs. Part of the floor was occupied by a table saw, a standing drill press, a band saw, and a wood lathe. A circuit breaker box on a separate line from the house held the 220 service he had run to power the tools. Another wall had bins for hand tools and their attachments: drills, routers, saws, and sanders. The center of the floor remained open, with enough room to pull in any of his or Fern's vehicles in case they needed repair.

Merry called it her dad's Batcave, and though it was a joke on her part, this shed did contain many of the secrets Levon wanted to hide from prying eyes. He entered the workshop through a man door set beside the big roll-up doors that ran across the entire front of the building. He secured the walk-in door with a pair of sliding bolts before flipping the switch that turned on the banks of LED lights mounted to the ceiling. The air still held the oily tang of gun-cleaning fluid from the work he'd done on the Hawkens.

A recent addition to the shop was a computer station with a PC tower and a pair of monitors, a mouse, and a keyboard. It was an off-grid unit with no modem and no connection to the internet. Levon booted it up, and while waiting, filled a percolator with cold water at the wash sink set in the corner. He spooned Maxwell House into the steel filter and started the coffee brewing.

Operating—even purchasing—a computer had required a steep learning curve to bring him up to speed on tech. It was an education he preferred to keep to himself, although Merry, like anyone born after 2000, was far more conversant with computers than he could ever hope to be. For her, it was intuitive. For him, it was a chore, but if he asked her advice, she'd become curious as to what he was up to, and he had no ready story for his sudden interest in IT.

That meant days spent in the library at the county seat, using their public internet access to learn what equipment he would need and how to use it. He bought the units at a Best Buy in Haley using cash.

The purpose of this crash course was the boxes of videotapes he'd taken from the home of Daniel "Dads" Sherwood back in the fall. There were hundreds of tapes going back a decade or more. They'd been recorded without the knowledge of Sherwood's clients, pedophiles who paid him for the use of the underage boys the former football coach kept captive in his remote farmhouse in the rural western end of the county. Sherwood, Levon presumed, had kept this secret collection of tapes for purposes of blackmail or maybe as protection from prosecution.

There were certainly enough highly placed men featured in the tapes, like the Georgia state representative who was visiting the house the night Levon arrived. Levon had been looking for his lost second cousin,

Trevor, only to find him in a basement graveyard with other abducted boys. The politician had died that night, along with his state trooper bodyguard and a couple others of the house's "guests." Dads Sherwood had died as well. Levon had left no one behind except the captive boys.

Seeing as how the actual events of that night had never made the newspaper or television, Levon knew the whole episode was being effectively covered up. There had been a few items buried in the county's newspaper about some "runaways" being recovered. The representative's death was explained as a single-car accident that had killed both him and the state trooper acting as his driver. He assumed there was an ongoing investigation into the evidence left behind at the Sherwood house, but it did not appear anywhere in the media. That had to be by design.

That was the primary reason Levon had taken the boxes of tapes with him that night. He had no faith that the powers that be would hand out any significant punishment to the men in the videos. The whitewashing of the state rep's death had confirmed that. The client list of the Sherwood house of horrors was being protected, out of fear of prosecution or partisan embarrassment, from any kind of public scrutiny. It didn't matter what the cause was. What it meant was that justice had not been served.

Not that Levon had a high regard for the concept of justice. In his experience, justice was a dangerous word, and he'd seen with his own eyes in hellholes all over the world what the pursuit of it could mean. Mostly, it was about settling scores, real or imagined.

What concerned him more was knowing that Dads Sherwood had been part of something bigger, something rotten hidden just out of sight. That something threatened innocents and children, and because there wasn't either the will or the desire on the part of those tasked with their protection to do a damned thing, those children continued to be used by vile men.

Or perhaps it was more insidious than that. Maybe there were enough powerful men in government with enough influence to run interference for the predators. Levon didn't know what could make a man that weak, that morally bankrupt. Perhaps it was a way to maintain their position of power. Perhaps they were abusers too. In the end, it was all the same. Kids were being hurt, and no one was looking out for them.

All Levon knew was what he'd learned in war, and he was applying that knowledge here.

The problem, essentially, was defeating an insurgency. The ring of abusers, of which Sherwood was only a part, was akin to a guerrilla force hiding among the population. Any counter-insurgency operation was all about intelligence, patience, and applying the proper amount of pressure to weak points in an effort to force the insurgents to break cover.

To make mistakes.

To step into the clear, where they could be eliminated.

He'd made a few forays based on the names he had, and since the fall, had been working on building a profile of the enemy.

Few of these efforts had paid off. They hadn't led him any farther up the chain. He wasn't after soldiers. He wanted generals.

Levon wasn't sure what the endgame would turn out to be. He had a vague strategy of creating a big enough stink that law enforcement agencies would be forced to act more aggressively. He'd do that by revealing evidence that could not be ignored.

That was where the tapes came in.

Once he'd assembled the proper gear and become adept at its use, he'd transferred all the tapes onto an external hard drive. He'd cataloged each tape according to the labels Dads had placed on them. Each had a name and date written on it in the same neat block lettering. The dates went back to the late nineties. On some, the full name was included, but on many, the coach had used codenames like Zorro, Cowboy Bill, or El Capitan. Levon had then wiped the tapes with a magnet before hauling them to the county landfill.

He'd started by comparing the names against the public records for convicted sex offenders and built a list of names from the matches. He'd then picked a few names at random and contacted them by phone, using one of a dozen burner phones he'd bought at a Walmart in Huntsville. The men he'd spoken to had been wary about talking to him, and most had hung up on him when he got to the subject of the procuring or offer of children. He'd kept making calls until he got to Edward Reisinger of Tuscaloosa, who, using loosely coded language and innuendo, had agreed to meet Levon to meet "someone new." According to his entry on city-file.com, Reisinger was a registered child molester and had two convictions for sexual assault and statutory rape. Two of his victims were his own sister's children, a boy of six and a girl of eleven.

Reisinger was an unemployed car salesman by trade, and it wasn't hard to see why he was out of work. He'd arrived at Levon's cabin at the Hideaway Inn off 65 well on his way to a stumbling drunk. Reisinger hadn't appeared to be very sharp even when sober, though his alcoholic haze had cleared a bit when he'd found himself duct-taped to a toilet in a stranger's bathroom.

Levon had asked him questions, and Reisinger had

explained in detail how contacts were made in his world through the use of a number of websites that appeared at first glance to be innocent. He'd supplied definitions of the common terms and code words used by network insiders. The kind of information offered by Reisinger would help him immerse himself in the shared community of child predators and traffickers.

When he'd wrung all there was out of Reisinger, he'd shot him through the chest and head with a .38. He'd disassembled the pistol and tossed it into the Tennessee River on his way home.

This was the knowledge he'd needed to fill in the gaps in his intelligence profiles.

Like the name of the man in the images Levon had shown Alexander Krogstad on the smartphone.

According to the tape label, the man in the video with the unidentified boy was "Champ." The video had been taken sixteen years earlier, but Krogstad had been able to identify him before slipping into a stupor and succumbing to the killing cold of the icy water.

After the computer booted, Levon sipped coffee as he froze images on Champ's tape to isolate the man's face. He used programs to clean up and enhance the images as best he could before transferring them to an encrypted file on the SD card in his phone.

He paid little attention to the news, so Champ's real name meant nothing to Levon. Since joining the Marines, he had tended to see life as a mission or a series of goals and deadlines. His years of training and service had only sharpened this fixation. He tended to discard any information that was not relevant to the task at hand.

That applied to every aspect of his life, down to home repairs or making sure the girls did their homework. He was not a regular consumer of news or entertainment since it didn't impact him directly. Mostly, he had no use for it. He'd sit with the girls to watch a movie or a TV show, but it was because he enjoyed being in their company. He derived pleasure from watching them react to what was on the screen. He would let his mind wander while, to them, he appeared to be enjoying the story.

Because of this intentional cognitive dissonance, it was only upon looking the name up in the library that he'd learned who the man was.

This man, this target, would be a challenge.

Levon would have to step back and give himself time to work out the proper angle of attack before he could even think of entering Champ's corner of the jungle.

7

Other than an imagined image of a kind of Amazon cop, a cross between Rhonda Rousey and Xena: Warrior Princess, Lindsay Dauber wasn't sure what to expect with the arrival of US Marshal Laura Strand.

What she did *not* expect was a petite 5' 5" in heels black woman wearing lollypop glasses that subtracted ten years from her age. On the phone, Marshal Strand had sounded a good foot taller and wider and several shades whiter. There had been steel behind that polite demeanor that Dauber had mistakenly translated into heft, and the marshal's mid-Atlantic accent, which was no accent at all, had thrown her way off the mark.

Making up for what Strand lacked in body mass was Marshal Vince Holland, who had the build of a competitive bodybuilder and the bearing, demeanor, and buzzcut of an ex-military man. The guy looked like someone had squeezed a Viking into a business suit. Lindsay thought she might just be in love.

After the introductions were made, Marshal Strand asked, "Is there a secure room we can use?"

Cy Godshall led the way to a windowless conference

room that sometimes doubled as an interrogation room. The two marshals took one side of the table and the GBI agents the other. Marshal Strand slid a laptop from a canvas case and spun it up.

"We have reason to believe, strongly believe, that a recent homicide you're working ties into a pattern of similar murders all over the southeast," Laura said as she tapped keys, eyes locked on the screen. Marshal Thor sat contemplating the universe in silence.

"You mean, specifically, this Krogstad fella?" Godshall asked.

"Yes, specifically." Laura turned the laptop so Godshall and Dauber could see the screen.

It showed a grid of eight photos, a mix of mug shots and family photos, all male. The last one on the bottom row was Krogstad's morgue photo. The GBI agents leaned in to look closer. Laura read from a typed sheet she'd taken from a pocket in her case.

"We see similarities in seven other cases. Birmingham and Huntsville in Alabama. Rocky Mount, North Carolina. Knoxville, Tennessee. Gainesville, Florida. And Athens and Valdosta in Georgia, as well as your latest in Pickens County."

"Similarities in what way?" Godshall asked.

"All of the victims were either murdered or their bodies disposed of within a half-day's drive of their homes. They had traveled alone to the place where they were killed. In each case, their cars were found within a half-mile or less from where their bodies were discovered."

"What does that tell you?" Marshal Holland asked in a tone like a jock doing color commentary on ESPN.

"They were lured to their deaths," Dauber said. When the big marshal gave her an approving nod, she flushed.

"What kind of timeline are we looking at?" Godshall asked.

"Since late September," Laura said.

"Well, this boy sure works fast," Godshall said with a whistle.

"That's why we think it's safe to rule these out as serial killings," Laura said. "Eight victims in less than four months doesn't match any known profile. These are classified as pattern crimes and will remain so in all communications. You understand why."

"So the federal bureau doesn't take an interest," Godshall said.

The marshals nodded.

The last thing anyone wanted in a hot ongoing homicide investigation was the FBI showing up to slow-walk the investigation. Their consultants from VICAP would go over the case with a microscope in the hope of catching a serial killer with some psychobabble hocuspocus that would sound good at a press conference that might take place ten years after the perpetrator had died of old age. What on God's green earth did that gang of lawyers know about working a homicide case?

"Do the MOs line up?" Dauber asked.

"Your victim is the second to die from hypothermia, in much the same way as…" Laura scanned her cheat sheet, "Walter Amis in Gainesville. He died at a Hampton Inn two weeks ago."

"And the others?"

Laura ran a finger down her list.

"Birmingham, Rocky Mount, and Knoxville by firearm. .38 Special in Alabama and Carolina. Two *different* thirty-eights. A 9mm in Tennessee. Blunt force trauma in Huntsville. Suffocation in Athens. And in Valdosta, we found the victim beaten to death in his own car."

"Beaten with what?"

"Fists. And no DNA. Chemical analysis of the wounds shows the killer wore vinyl gloves, a heavy ply available at any Home Depot."

"This is one pissed-off sumbitch," Godshall said.

"No. I don't think that's the case," Laura said. "Each of these killings was methodical. This guy takes every measure not to leave behind even a bit of useable evidence. And no witnesses."

"It's as if he's hunting them," Holland put in. "And when he catches them? It's lights out. I doubt most of them saw it coming. He doesn't play with his food like a psycho would."

"They're more like executions," Laura said. "Precise. This guy knows how to kill and does it quickly with little or no mess."

"That says 'military' to me," Godshall said.

Both marshals nodded.

"Okay, he's the Terminator. Except for the ones he made into popsicles," Dauber said.

"That's thrown us a curve," Laura said. "That's one of the reasons we're looking for your help."

"This old boy was looking for something. Or someone. Or some damn information about some damn thing," Godshall said.

"What can you tell us about this Krogstad?" Laura asked, fingers poised over the keys of her laptop.

"He was a baby-raper," Dauber said. "He did time and is in the registry."

"Where's that fit into your pattern?" Godshall asked.

"Like pocket aces," Marshal Holland said with a feral leer that brought a dew of sweat to the backs of Lindsay Dauber's knees.

"Well, let's see about filling out that hand for you,

son," Godshall said and patted the tabletop with his palm.

8

The half-moon hung over the treetops in a clear sky, its blue-gray glow reflecting off the fresh snowfall. Levon drove the Avalanche up the packed gravel drive with its headlights off. The indigo shadows the trees cast over the hummocks of snow made it feel as though he were driving his truck across the floor of a luminous ocean.

The rutted drive climbed gradually to the top of a knob of ground, where it flattened out in a broad area dotted with low-roofed cabins. It had once been a Boy Scout camp but was long abandoned. Where there were once neatly delineated walkways of chipped pine shavings lined with whitewashed rocks, there was now a dense carpet of ferns crushed by the weight of the snow. The dark shapes of the cabins looked adrift atop them.

Levon pulled alongside a cabin and killed the engine. He sat there in the dark while cold crept into the cab, his head back against the rest and his eyes closed. His mental clock was set for one hour, something he'd been trained to do by Gunny Leffertz back in SERE. He recalled laughing at the idea when it was explained to him, but Gunny hadn't laughed and had told him he needed to forget the impossible and open his mind to the possible.

"All this high livin' and cushy bullshit comfort has bred the animal out of you, son," Gunny had said to him. "You and me come from different tribes, but there was a time both our people waited out the night with a spear in their hands and eyes on the dark. They could *feel* that dark. Shit, they could feel the *stars* passing by over them. They were in touch. We all *lost* that, and we need to get it back. You think *I'm* blind? Most folks are walkin' around with their heads up their asses and no idea what's looking at them from out of the dark."

If he was to see in the dark, Levon would need his night vision. An hour with his eyes closed here in the cold would give him distance and clarity in the light of the moon.

He needed this time alone to sort his thoughts. This task he'd set himself, the men on those tapes, was troubling him. He wondered for the hundredth time if he should have left those tapes where he found them. If he should have let the law take its course. Only there was no guarantee of that.

Here in the cold and the dark, miles from home and alone with only his mind for company, Levon knew he needed this. He needed the focus, the purpose, of the hunt.

At the end of one hour, he eased the cab door open. His boots made a crunching sound as they broke the fresh rime of ice covering the snow. He opened the rear door to drop the seatback. A shotgun and a rifle hung in a rack. He chose the rifle, a modified M-1 carbine.

He walked south away from the truck to the rear of the scout camp, where the ground dropped away into a deep holler. This was the next holler over and to the north from where someone had shot a rifle at him and Merry. Levon knew it from hunting here in his youth. It was a blind gulch ending in a bowl-shaped depression enclosed by steep inclines. The neck of the holler was made impassable by a thick growth of berries and thorn, rough country for a man but heaven for deer and other game. He and his brother Dale had only hunted here once and had found it an unforgiving place.

Through a starlight monocular, he viewed the drop below. The lenses turned the blackness to an alien landscape of green and gray shimmering under the moonlight. There was no movement. Nothing he could see. Plenty to feel, though. The darkness below was alive with something.

Levon picked the easiest grade off the ridge and made his way down to the floor of the holler. He took his time, taking care not to make noise, but when it could not be avoided, matching his movements to the sounds made by the wind through the treetops. The creaks and groans of the branches were a screen for his footfalls.

Another peek through the starlight scope revealed a trail. He followed its serpentine path as it tracked back and forth along ledges of more level ground that led in natural steps down to the bottomland.

There was a slight tang of woodsmoke in the air. He came to a halt in the shadow of a massive boulder at the base of the ridge. He scanned the dense growth of birches and hackberry with the monocular but saw no source of light that would mean a campfire. The direction of the wind was no help since the deepening cold of the night was drawing down air from the ridges that walled the holler.

He waited in the shelter of the stone with his eyes,

ears, and mind open. An hour had passed when the wind shifted in a dominant westerly gust. It carried the smoke scent to him, stronger now. The fire lay in the blind end of the holler to the west.

Placing his feet with care, Levon made his way toward the source of the smoke. It grew more pronounced as he moved west. He pinpointed the general direction of the fire and made sure to keep the trees between him and where he suspected it to be. Anyone watching from cover would be looking for movement. He made certain to use the silhouettes of the trees to conceal his approach, adjusting his path to move under older growth where the ground was clearer of brush.

Dropping to one knee, he unslung the carbine from his shoulder before taking a look around the bole of an ancient elm. Peering first with his naked eyes, Levon scanned the way ahead for signs of smoke and saw a thin finger of white smoke rising above a tangle of sumac. The wind dispersed it as it rose through the branches. Next, he looked hard at the base of the trees for a shape, movement, or any other anomaly that did not belong.

A hummock was visible through the skein of trees. It was too regular and geometric to be a boulder or a dirt mound or any other natural formation. Levon switched to the monocular and saw the shape was a tent of some kind.

It was a dome-shaped tent covered with a second layer of a tarp in a camouflage pattern. The tendril of smoke rose from a firepit set in some cleared ground before the tent opening. The pit was deep enough to hide the glow of the firelight. There was a folding camp stool by the fire, and now that he was closer, Levon caught the scent of roasted meat and cooked onions. A neat stack of cut wood in two cords at the edge of the clearing was proof that this was a permanent camp. All evidence pointed to a single camper.

Levon surveyed the ground that lay between him and the tent with greater care. The moonlight gleamed silver off a thin strand stretched between two trees at ankle height. Further searching revealed more lengths of fishing line strung taut all around the camp. Empty cans spaced three feet apart and presumably filled with pebbles hung from the lines. He looked for other such traps or warning devices but saw nothing more.

He slung the carbine back on his shoulder and reached through the handwarmer pocket of his farm coat for the .45 auto he wore in a clamshell holster on his belt. With the Colt held close to his body and trained at the tent, he made his way forward. Levon's eyes were locked on the tent except for brief looks along the edges and at the ground ahead. Anyone who'd hang a wake-up line might have tanglefoot traps set under the snow or ground cover.

As he closed on the camp, he saw it lacked the usual detritus that spread around a casual outing, especially a camp that had been made a long-term home as he suspected this one to be. There was a deerskin drying on a handmade willow rack. A line was slung between two trees, from which hung some socks to dry. A steel kettle for boiling water sat by the edge of the firepit. There was a watertight storage trunk of heavy plastic by the tent opening.

The snow before the tent opening, secured closed now, showed the clear impressions of boot soles. The prints were all around the fire pit and the woodpile. Another trail of prints led away from the camp into the trees.

Levon stopped twenty feet from the tent and listened,

the .45 held in both hands and aimed at the tent opening. He waited as the wind died down.

Through the winter quiet, in a moment of stillness, he could hear a rhythmic sound rising and falling through the ripstop nylon.

Someone inside was sound asleep.

And snoring.

9

"Don't move," Levon said, his voice low but firm.

The man in the tent rose suddenly from the folds of a heavy sleeping bag and blinked into the bar of moonlight that fell over him. He stopped, eyes on the barrel of the Colt aimed at his center mass in an unwavering grip.

He was a black man with a heavy beard, but his hair was close-cropped, roughly Levon's height, but with the thinner, leaner build of a man who was using himself up. It was hard to determine his age in the gloom, though he moved with the easy surety of a younger man.

Levon spared a glance around the tent. There was a backpack, some gallon water jugs, a pile of paperback books, and some neatly folded clothes in a basket woven from willow strips. Against the wall of the tent leaned a wood axe with a gleaming blade, as well as a bow saw. A toolbox in bright yellow plastic lay near these.

The black shape of an unadorned AR-15 lay within easy reach on the baby-blue foam pad under the man's sleeping bag. The man made no move to reach for it, though it was clear from his eyes that he was strongly inclined to do so.

"Hands," Levon said.

The man showed his hands.

"Sit up," Levon said. "Slow."

The man did so.

"Draw your legs out."

The man drew his legs up to his chest and free of the sleeping bag. One of his legs was of gleaming high-tensile steel from mid-calf down and ended in a high-impact plastic foot. He sat like that, palms forward and hands spread. He was wearing boxers and a t-shirt that was once white.

"Pull some pants on."

The man reached for a pair of khaki pants lying by the bag. There was a clasp knife with a four-inch blade clipped to a belt on the khakis. Something would have to be done about that, but not now, Levon thought. He could tell from the man's eyes that he was taking the threat of the Colt seriously. If he had any doubts, the icy stillness in Levon's eyes had dispelled them.

Levon took a half-step back into the moonlight.

"On your feet," he said once the man had the khakis pulled up and buttoned. "You can touch the tent ceiling if you need to."

The threat was implicit. Drop a hand lower than your shoulder and pay the price.

The man rose easily, eyes on Levon the whole time, without the need for support. He ducked to step out of the tent, following Levon, who was backing into the open. When he had stepped well clear, Levon moved around him and stopped when his back was to the tent, between the man and his weapon. He assessed the man more closely now.

He was few inches shorter than Levon. He looked fit enough and healthy enough, though he was underweight by a good twenty pounds. He was no tweaker or junkie.

His eyes were clear in the moonlight and studying Levon. The eyes betrayed no anger or fear, just cool appraisal, a bit of curiosity, and perhaps a touch of regret at being taken in his sleep. He glanced around to determine that Levon was alone.

"You got coffee?" Levon asked.

The man blinked at him in surprise.

"Some," the man said. Even in that one-word reply, Levon could hear the drawl.

"Make us some."

"Only got one cup." Tennessee accent. Middle Tennessee was Levon's guess.

"We'll share."

"Can I put my boots on?"

"Sure. Only don't lace them."

Only after Levon had nodded his assurance did the man move to pull a pair of well-maintained but well-worn leather boots from where they had been placed upside-down on a pair of stakes driven into the dirt near the tent opening. Levon covered him back to the fire, where the man sat on the camp stool to pull the boots on over the woolen sock of one foot and the bare plastic of the other. He then set to work filling his steel kettle from a jug after dropping a few fresh chunks of cut wood atop the smoldering fire. Levon gestured him back to the camp stool.

"What's your name?" Levon asked. He took a seat on the storage trunk, the Colt resting on his knee.

"Wesley Tyler Ruskin," the man said.

"What branch were you in?"

"Army." If he was surprised at the question, Wesley Ruskin did not show it.

"What was your MOS?"

"11-C. Combat engineer."

"What unit?"

"Company C, 3rd Battalion, 8th Cav."

"Iraq?"

"Yeah. Two deployments."

"First or second Fallujah?"

"Second. Part of the surge. You there?"

"March 2004."

"Bullshit. First battle was in April."

"Someone had to go in ahead of y'all."

Wesley gave Levon a harder look before glancing away.

"So, what we do now?" Wesley asked.

"That was you took a shot at my daughter and me." Levon's voice was flat and even, no trace of anger or resentment.

"Didn't know that was a girl."

"Would it have made a difference?"

Wesley shrugged.

The steel kettle burbled, and they both looked at it. The spout was spitting steaming droplets into the fire, where they hissed.

"You're sittin' on the coffee," Wesley said, nodding at the trunk under Levon.

He stood and undid the clasps to open the trunk with one hand. A can of Folgers sat atop resealable sacks of rice, beans, and flour. He tossed the coffee to Wesley, who, using a flap of deer hide to protect his hand, poured a steel mug full of boiling water and tipped coffee in from the can. He offered his guest the mug, but Levon gestured for him to take the first drink.

"Like I asked, what do we do now?" Wesley asked after his first tenuous sip of the scalding brew.

"I'm thinking that's up to you," Levon said.

"Say what?" Wesley was perplexed, with a tinge of impatience in his voice.

"You been up in this holler a year or more. Before

that, you were somewhere that didn't suit you. Maybe you got in some trouble. Maybe you just chucked it in and came here to clear your head, and when that didn't work, maybe you decided you belong up here."

"You know a whole shitload about me, huh?"

"I know what I see. I've seen a lot of the same shit you've seen."

"That make us brothers?" Wesley's impatience had turned to scorn.

"All I'm saying is, I've been where you are."

"Where's that?"

"Coming home and spending months drugged up on painkillers. Then back to a life you barely remember with more drugs to help you cope. Walking around looking at life through the wrong end of the scope like everyone, and everything is right there but out of your reach. After a while, even the drugs don't help you sleep. You spend your nights feeling angry or scared and your days feeling hollow inside."

The edge came off Wesley's hard gaze, but his lips remained turned up in a smirk.

"And you're gonna tell me how you got past all that."

"Naw. I'm still working that shit out myself. I'm not here to teach you the way out. Just sharing, I guess."

"I wanted to *feel* something, you know?" Wesley lowered his gaze to the ground, looking through the steam rising from the mug resting on his knee.

"It's not enough. That I *can* tell you." Levon stooped forward to take the mug from his hand, then sat back down and took a long draw of the hot, rich coffee.

"I guess. But stayin' in Pulaski wasn't workin' for me."

"You stay up here, and chances are you'll get sick or injured and the coyotes'll eat you."

"Or some redneck motherfucker will come up here

and put a bullet in me." There was a trace of a smile in the words.

"Or some hillbilly motherfucker. Or an asshole down from Nashville on a long weekend from his law firm."

Wesley made a *pfft* sound with his lips.

"Well, thanks for the coffee." Levon rose to his feet and handed the mug back.

Wesley watched Levon open the farm coat to return the automatic to its holster.

"You might want to pile some more brush around the tent. I picked it out even in the dark." Levon turned and walked east into the trees.

Wesley watched him step over the trap lines and make his way toward the sumacs.

"I never meant to hit y'all," he called after the man moving away into the gloom.

"I know that," Levon replied, invisible in the dark.

10

Champ had a politician's smile, as empty as the promise behind it.

In a studio pose, the face of a man in his early forties beamed from the monitor on several websites. Sometimes in a suit and tie, sometimes in an open-collar dress shirt. Sometimes with a carefully trimmed goatee, sometimes with his chin bare. But always the same fixed "so glad to see you" expression of satisfaction and welcome. There were a few pictures of him posing like a proud uncle with small children at Little League and youth soccer events.

Levon hunched over a keyboard that sat before a row of monitors n the main room of the library. Other patrons were busy at their own computers along the row. A pair of teenagers stifled giggles over something they'd pulled up. An older gentleman played some kind of animated game with balls and gems.

Justin Hicks was the name given to him by the man in the tub at the Cedar Ridge Motor Lodge. It had taken some time to connect the name to a series of child place-ment services in Limestone, Madison, and Marshall County in the northeast corner of the state. Hicks was a lawyer with a degree from Loyola who'd passed the Alabama and Georgia bars eighteen years ago. He was currently the lead attorney of an agency called Heart and Home, an LLC incorporated in Nevada, with its home office in the Brookhurst section of Huntsville. He was on the board of several other agencies in that part of the state and had won several awards from church groups and non-profits, including a humanitarian award from the Department of Children and Families for Region Three.

Anyone reading his history of helping to find homes for unwanted children and the stories of his "caring and compassion" would have a hard time recognizing the man in the unlabeled video footage Levon had found in the locked room at Dads Sherwood's house. As evidenced by the dates on the video labels spread across more than a decade and dozens of different victims, Hicks had been a frequent visitor to the house. No doubt in Levon's mind that a lot of the boys seen in those videos were among the remains he'd found buried in the cellar under the Sherwood farmhouse.

That was why none of his tapes were labeled. He was a regular, maybe even in business with Sherwood. He wouldn't be a subject for blackmail, but Sherwood would still want something on his partner in case he ever had need of it.

"You interested in adoption?"

Levon turned from the screen. One of the library workers, a reed-thin woman in her forties, was standing behind him with an armful of magazines in plastic covers.

"My wife and I are considering it," he said.

"You'd need an agency in our county." She nodded at

the screen displaying the home page of the child place-ment agency in Huntsville. "You'd do better looking at one in Haley."

"Guess I followed the wrong link," Levon said, returning to the screen.

"Happens to me," she said. She ambled toward the racks of periodicals. "Clickbait."

He waited until she was occupied, her back turned, replacing magazines on the standing racks before getting up to leave.

This library was no good to him anymore. He'd been here often enough to be noticed and for a worker to feel familiar enough to remark on his presence. He'd have to drive farther now. Maybe a library in a bigger city like Huntsville since it looked like he'd be traveling there soon.

For now, he had what he needed.

It was time to meet Uncle Fern.

———

"I'LL BE with you in just a moment," the skinny redhead assured them for the second time before stepping back into her glass-walled office and closing the door.

Levon and Fern Cade sat on a lemon-yellow faux leather bench in the waiting area of the lobby of the Southway's Bank branch in Haley. A thick paper folder bound with steel clips rested on the cushion between them.

"You coulda worn something more businesslike," Fern groused. He was dressed in what he called his funeral suit, with a white shirt and a paisley tie. It hung loose on him due to the weight he'd lost following his recent gallbladder surgery.

"They're not gonna lend us money based on what

clothes we're wearing," Levon said. He was, as usual, in his work boots, jeans, cotton shirt, and barn coat.

"It mighta helped some." Fern feigned interest in a folder about retirement options that had a white-haired couple kayaking through whitewater rapids on the cover.

"We have more than enough collateral to secure the loan. Besides, if they turn us down, I can cover the start-up costs."

"That wasn't the deal, nephew." Fern leaned closer, lowering his voice. "You need something to show on a tax return. That's the whole idea behind this."

"That and getting you into the liquor business legal for once."

Fern made a *feh* sound and returned to pretending to read about investment accounts for seniors. Levon watched the traffic on the highway through the two-story window wall that fronted the bank.

The skinny redhead stepped out of her office again and held the door for an elderly gentleman with a tripod-based walking cane who was helped along by a woman, presumably his daughter. Neither looked like they'd be going kayaking this afternoon. After goodbyes and assurances, the redhead turned her professional smile on Levon and Fern.

"Gentlemen?" she called and gestured for them to step into her lair.

The loan manager, Karen Witcomb-Reese, looked over the business plan laid out on her desktop. It had been prepared with the help of Merry and had the look of a professional presentation. There was even a rough sketch of the proposed company logo for Blue Moon Whiskey, featuring a blue crescent moon shining over pine tops. Ms. Witcomb-Reese showed more interest in the list of collateral possessions than in the proposal and pie charts.

"You own this property outside Colby outright?" she asked.

"That note was paid off by my daddy, Levon's grand-daddy, after he come back from fighting the Germans," Fern assured her. "It's an improved property with some new outbuildings and fencing. It's all there in the county assessment."

"And these vehicles? You have the titles for them?"

Fern nodded. "Free and clear, ma'am."

"I see that neither of you is currently employed."

"That's true, ma'am. That's true. But me and my nephew both get regular checks from the VA as we're veterans."

"You're looking to borrow close to two hundred thousand dollars."

"Yes, ma'am." Fern leaned from his guest chair to point at the papers spread across the desk. "We're planning on leasing an empty garage building in Colby for our distillery. We need money to clean that place up to the health codes, then there's equipment, bottles, labels, advertising, and such as that."

"You'll be several months setting up this operation before making any actual sales?"

"Well, we don't plan on offering aged corn liquor at first, but we'll need some time to set up the vats for fermentation and like that."

"How will you meet the initial monthly payments?"

"We read in your brochures about something called a grace period to give us time to get on our feet, so to speak?

"The bank would need some assurances that you would be able to make your monthly payments on schedule." The redhead's mercenary smile was more brittle now.

Levon made a growling noise, and both Fern and Ms. Whitcomb-Reese turned to him. It was the first utterance either had heard from him since they'd all taken seats.

"What if we were to open an account here against the loan?" he asked. "It would be there as a guarantee that we had the funds needed to meet the note."

"Well, I suppose that would go a long way to seeing this application approved."

"My uncle can come in tomorrow and open a business account that you can include with other collateral. Would eight thousand cover us for the first three months?"

The gusto returned to the redhead's smile.

———

OUT IN THE PARKING LOT, Fern walked with Levon to where their trucks were parked side by side.

"Where'd you come up with eight thousand?" Fern asked.

"Hell, Fern, I have that much on me," Levon said as he started his truck with the remote.

"I mean the figure. Why eight thousand?"

"Because if it's ten, then they have to report it to the IRS right away. And if I said nine thousand, it might make her think we're purposely dodging the taxman."

"They teach you that devious shit in the Corps?"

"That and other places." Levon slid behind the wheel of his Avalanche.

"You going home?"

"I'll be a bit behind you. I promised the girls

Wendy's." Levon closed his door and backed out into the lot.

Fern Cade watched his nephew ease into the midday traffic before getting into the cab of his truck to head home.

11

When she was fully armored, Laura Strand always felt like one of those geeks at a comic book convention playing dress-up. But the marshals required it on raids, even if she wasn't going to be charging through the door with the alpha dogs. At least suiting up was keeping her warm in the late December chill.

They were staged along a country road a half-mile from their target, a trailer in a park called Willow Run fifteen miles north of Huntsville, Alabama. The sun was a few hours from coming up, and there was a nip in the air she could feel even packed into the unmarked Suburban with four other marshals in green BDUs, helmets, and body armor. A second Suburban was parked behind them, with three more marshals inside. Four state trooper cruisers and a Madison County sheriff's car were here as well, lights off. They were here to show support and help with any unforeseen complications that might crop up.

Their investigation into a few of the recent sex offenders found murdered across the region had borne fruit. Two of the victims had had recent and frequent telephone contact with one Oscar Raymond Cruz, who claimed a duplex in Hillendale as his primary residence. The property tax rolls also revealed his ownership of a thirty-foot Coachman at Willow Run. Simultaneous raids on both properties were set for five AM, ten minutes from now. The raid on the duplex was being honchoed by Vince Holland.

Mr. Cruz was a repeat sex offender with a long history of child endangerment, sexual contact with a minor, and aggravated assault. His record of convictions, incarcerations, and acquittals was filled with multiple offenses across Georgia, Florida, and South Carolina. Seven years before, he'd narrowly skated from a human trafficking charge in Arizona on a bonehead technicality. On paper, he'd been clean since then. On paper.

He could be their man in the recent multiple murders of baby-rapers, though Laura strongly doubted it. More likely, he was part of a network that two of the victims belonged to. Associations between pedophiles were Byzantine and formed Venn diagrams with dozens of circles that intersected online, in person, and by phone.

Having Cruz's name and number come up again and again in the call records of burner phones found in searches of the two victims' homes had put him on the fast track for a no-knock visit. What had clinched the deal and made a judge sign off on the warrant were the frequent sightings of unattended kids entering, and apparently living, in the Coachman trailer without adult supervision.

In the past two days, she had observed, from the concealment of an unoccupied trailer with a view of the Cruz trailer, kids treating Willow Run as their home. Three kids, two girls and a boy, one who looked to be as young as seven, had played on swings at the park's playground and ridden bikes down to the Circle K a half-mile distant. It looked like kids off from school on Christmas break, only there were no signs of grownups in residence, and the kids had about them the woebegone look of refugees. Unlaundered clothes and dirty hands. After four days of stakeout, the graveyard watch had observed Cruz's 2010 Lexus pulling into the trailer park. The warrant had been obtained, and now they were waiting to jump off.

"Time," she said.

"Nut up, everyone," the marshal behind the wheel added.

The big SUVs revved their engines, and Laura rolled down her passenger side window to wave her hand in a circle to the state and county cars. They were on radio silence since these serial pervs listened to police frequencies like they were Top 40.

The Suburbans hurtled forward and swung hard into the trailer park, spraying gravel. They came to juddering halts before the target Coachman. Brilliant searchlights mounted on the cars threw the trailer into sudden daylight. The cars rocked as the burly marshals exited, rifles and shotguns raised. Laura's glasses steamed with condensation when she stepped out of the muggy warmth of the SUV cabin into the frigid air.

No words were spoken because none were needed. The lead marshal tore off the screen door with a pry bar and allowed the number two man to throw a shoulder against the flimsy steel inner door, sending it crashing inward.

Shouts of "US marshals!" rang out as the four marshals entered. The other three covered the windows on all sides of the long trailer, now yawing on its wheels and stands like a ship at sea. Laura worried that it might tip over.

Muffled pops sounded from inside, followed by the

throaty roar of a shotgun. A high keening grew louder when a window at the front end of the trailer was thrust open. Laura joined two marshals there, her sidearm unholstered and ready.

A little girl, the youngest of the trio they'd observed, was trying to escape through the narrow window. Blunt-cut hair the color of honey, her staring eyes were made to appear wider by the rings of heavy mascara around them. Her mouth looked like a wound, smeared with bright red lipstick. The bruises on her thin arms showed livid in the harsh light from the searchlights. She wore only panties and an outsized pair of cowboy boots. She was the source of the screaming, a quavering animal cry of fear.

Oscar Raymond Cruz had foolishly opted to resist arrest, taking several shots at the marshals with a revolver he'd pulled out from under a waterbed. Two of the shots had gone into the ceiling. A third had blasted a hole in the bed, creating a spout of water. The lead marshal took Cruz center mass with a load of buck that threw the man into the faux panel wall. The little girl in the cowboy boots was the only other occupant of the room, and she had attempted to escape the noise and the smell of fresh blood.

The other two kids, a girl and boy, both eleven, were wakened from where they slept in a fold-out cot in the trailer's living room. The girl was a light-skinned African-American. The boy looked Latino. They obeyed the marshal's orders and were removed from the trailer and taken to the warmth of one of the Suburbans, where Laura joined them. The screaming little girl was brought over as well, quieter now, face white with shock.

"You're all right now," Laura said, fighting to keep her voice even. "We're with the Missing Child Unit. You'll stay with me until we can get you to where some doctors and nurses can take a look at you."

All three kids showed bruising and open scabs on their bare legs and arms. The oldest girl had a poorly healed cigarette burn on one forearm.

"Will the doctors hurt us?" the oldest girl said, her arm around the smaller girl to quiet her.

"No. No one is going to hurt you."

"That's what they always say," the older girl said.

"That's what who says?" Laura asked.

"Uncle Oscar and his friends."

12

The trailer raid netted almost zero useable data. It had yielded the rescue of three at-risk kids and the erasure of a useless piece of human debris from this mortal coil. It was clear that the trailer served as a holding pen for the captive kids as well as a playhouse for Cruz's sick pursuits.

The duplex in Hillendale was another story.

That place was a goldmine.

Oscar Cruz lived in one half of the modest three-bedroom with his common-law wife, Raquel. The other side of it was home to his unmarried sister-in-law, Janine, and her two kids. From interviews with the sisters, it was a partly open marriage, with the two women sharing Cruz as a husband.

Cruz's office had a heavily encrypted computer setup with multiple external hard drives. That would be boxed up and sent to Washington to be cracked. The marshals found a plastic container concealed in an attic space that was packed with DVD-Rs loaded with thousands of hours of kiddie porn. That was enough cause to arrest the sisters and charge them with possession of child pornography under 18 USC §2251 and allowed them to remand the two kids in residence to the county court, along with charging Janine with child endangerment by allowing her minor children to share a residence with a registered sex offender. They'd leave it to the federal prosecutors to prove the duplex was a shared residence.

That was all the legal niceties sorted, with a bonanza of evidence to follow once the techies cracked Cruz's passwords.

It left the harder part of the job for Laura.

Regrettably, the only place to house the three kids taken from the trailer the night before was in the Neaves-Davis Center for Children. It was a detention center for juvenile offenders. There was a special protective wing where each kid was given their own room, separate from the general population.

Laura would interview each of the kids individually with a juvie matron and a child advocate assigned under Alabama state law. She met the matron, Miss Summers, a heavy-set black woman who looked as if she wouldn't even know how to begin taking shit from anyone. The child advocate was a tiny white woman named Betsy Ritter, with red-rimmed eyes behind reading glasses. Laura suspected she was a stoner until she decided the woman was probably an insomniac. It was a better fit given a career dealing with abused kids. Laura knew her own job in the Missing Children Unit had a burnout rate higher than air traffic controllers or ICU nurses.

With the matron and advocate seated on either side of her, Laura spoke to the three children individually. The boy was severely withdrawn and was only interested in whether or not he could watch the TV in the shared community area or go outside where he could hear other boys playing b-ball. Upon learning he could not do either, he lost interest in cooperating. The smallest of the three, determined to be an underdeveloped eight years old, most probably due to malnutrition, was either traumatized or developmentally challenged. She would not look Laura in the eye.

The oldest by two months over the boy was the light-skinned black girl. Her name was Nadine Halleck. She was the most talkative of the three, especially after being offered a bowl of ice cream from the center's kitchen.

Nadine had cleaned up, the bruises on her arms and legs covered by a simple cotton shirt and drawstring pants provided by the county. Her hair was shorter since they'd had to cut the mats out of it at the hospital where she'd been examined. The room smelled like the lice medication they'd washed her head with when she was admitted to the center.

"I was his favorite," she said between spoonfuls of ice cream. "Until that little blonde bitch come along."

"What made you his favorite?" Laura asked.

"He picked me most often to be with, and he hardly hit me no more."

"Did he bring other men to the trailer?"

"Sometimes."

"Do you know their names?"

"One's called Richie. I think he's Uncle Oscar's cousin. They kinda look alike. And another guy named Angel. He's Richie's friend."

"And they would be with you, too?"

"Sometimes. You got strawberry?" Nadine tilted the empty bowl at Laura.

"If you answer all my questions, all right?" Laura forced a smile. These questions and the answers were turning her stomach into a clenched fist.

"Okay."

"I don't have them now, but if I get pictures of this cousin, could you identify him?"

"Like on the TV? Oh, sure. He easy to pick out. Got a tattoo right here." She pointed to her cheek just below the corner of her eye.

"Is it a black teardrop?" A common prison tat.

"How you know that?"

"Wild guess."

"He look kinda like that Mexican guy plays Ant-Man's friend. In the movies."

"Okay. We'll have pictures for you later. You can show us."

"And ice cream?"

"I promised, didn't I?"

"Strawberry next time?"

"As long as you answer just a few more questions."

Nadine sat ready, hands folded before her in a caricature of an eager student. Her face was creased in a broad, tight-lipped smile, her eyes bright. The image made the fist in Nadine's stomach tighten.

"You were allowed outside. You could go to the park and down to the store."

"We done that sometimes."

"And you were allowed to do that? Anytime you liked?"

"Long as we were there when Uncle Oscar needed us to be. Long as we were back home before dark."

Home. The fist turned in her gut.

"Then why didn't you run away? Why didn't you leave and tell someone what Uncle Oscar was doing to you?"

Nadine blinked, perplexed.

"Run away where?"

"Anywhere. Somewhere safe."

Nadine scoffed, chin up and eyes closed.

"Ain't nowhere's safe. Ain't no one to tell gives a shit."

"Why not? You could have called the police or spoken

to a neighbor. There are people to look out for you like Miss Summers and Miss Ritter. Don't you have family?"

"Never had no family."

"Where were you before Uncle Oscar?"

"I was with a foster family over at Hazel Green. I was in one at Brownsboro before that, and in one off Bob Wallace before that."

"And Uncle Oscar took you from there?"

"Naw. Shit." Nadine shook her head. "You don't know shit, do you?"

"I won't know anything unless you tell me, Nadine."

"They sold me to Uncle Oscar. For money."

———

OUTSIDE IN THE PARKING LOT, Laura sucked in lungsful of cold air and blew them out slowly to make the knot in her stomach ease its grip. Ms. Ritter, the child advocate with the tired eyes, lit a Kool in cupped hands as she walked toward her from the guards' station.

"All three of those kids were in foster care," she said by way of greeting. "I'm having the files pulled. My guess is that the other two were sold to Cruz out of care too."

"This is a thing?" Laura said. "Kids sold out of foster homes for cash?"

"Sometimes it's barter. I had a foster parent last year trade a four-year-old for a season ticket to the Falcons."

"Jesus Christ."

"Look, I'm glad your department's giving this some attention." Betsy Ritter blew out a stream of smoke. "I only hope you're not all down here to make a show, take some pictures, and make it look like you've done something. 'Cause this system is broken. It's rotten. and there's damn-all the state can do to catch up, even if they wanted to."

"What are you saying?" Laura was taken aback by hearing words like this from a social worker.

"I'm saying, if you really want to make a difference here, you're gonna have to go to war."

Laura thought, *There might be someone out there doing just that.*

13

His beard crinkled with frost while Wesley Ruskin worked on dressing the buck. Vapor drifted from the warmth of the open carcass, which was split from throat to rump, the rib cage held open with a stick.

He'd hung it up the night before to let it bleed out into a pit he'd dug for the purpose. The pit was filled with dirt now to hide the guts, forelegs, hooves, and the scent of blood from the foxes and coyotes and wild dogs that roamed the ridges around the holler. He'd heard a bear once back in the summer and assumed it was off somewhere, napping through the cold.

"Hey," a voice called from the pines toward the foot of the gully. "I'm coming in. You hear me?"

"I hear you," Wesley called back.

The man who called himself Levon Cade emerged from the morning gloom with a pack over his shoulder. His hands were empty. No rifle.

"Big buck. That the same one my girl had in her sights?" he asked as he set the canvas pack down.

"Yeah. He's an old one. Thought I'd make way for a young buck to make his move, you know?" Wesley worked his curved skinning blade to peel back the hide, revealing lean muscles over ribs marbled with thin ripples of yellow fat.

"You're gonna have to let that soak awhile."

"I know. Old fella's gonna be gamey as hell. Got some wild onions, dried mustard. Ran outta vinegar a while back."

"Maybe this'll help." Levon rummaged through the pack and pulled out a bottle of red wine.

"That'll sure do. You always bring vino along when you hike?"

"This pack's not for me. It's for you. Brought you some clean socks, some Payday bars, some chocolate, salt, sugar, and a couple cans of coffee creamer."

"Why'd you do that?"

"So the next time I come up here, I don't have to drink that nasty-ass coffee of yours."

"I'm nobody to you." Wesley set his knife on a tarp next to his saw and a longer filleting knife.

"I live about ten miles that way." Levon nodded to the south. "No one lives between my back property line and here. We're practically neighbors."

"Then let me make you some coffee." Wesley reached for a stained strip of terry cloth to wipe his hands.

"I'll make it. You keep on trimmin' that buck."

Levon had brought a steel mug for himself and poured a serving of heavily sweetened and creamed coffee for each of them.

"Damn, that's good," Wesley said after draining his mug.

He returned to dressing the buck and Levon helped, holding the carcass from swinging while it was being hided. Once it was stripped of its skin, they hoisted it higher to keep it out of the reach of predators. It would hang there in the cold air for a week or more to age the meat properly.

They raised the buck out of reach and tied off the hoist line around a tree bole. Wesley asked, "You sure you don't want to take some home with you?"

"I might take a haunch next time I come up. You got a tub for marinating it?"

"I'll use my storage container like I done before." He nodded at the deerskin, which was now draped over his tent.

"Let me bring you something next time. A plastic tub."

Wesley took a seat, leaned against the trunk of a tree, and regarded Levon with narrowed eyes.

"Okay," Levon said as he felt through the main compartment of the pack. "We can talk about it over breakfast."

"You invitin' yourself to breakfast now?"

"No. I'm inviting *you*." Levon removed a carton of eggs, a plastic-wrapped pound of bacon, and a Tupperware tub of cooked grits.

———

THEY RAN the skillet and mess plates under water from a spring at the base of the holler. Wesley scrubbed them clean with a rough cloth while Levon dried.

"You have family?" Levon asked.

"My mom and dad in Murfreesboro. My sister's married and moved on up to Indiana. My brother-in-law's got a good job there with a drug company."

"You're not married?"

"Naw. Came close. When I got outta Walter Reed I come back home, only I didn't call her. What's she want with me now? Wakin' up the whole house most nights, screamin' and shit."

"You decide that on your own?"

"Yeah. She found out I was home. Came by a few times. I didn't want to see her. I ain't the man I was."

"Who is? My wife had to put up with a lot with me working through shit, but I couldn't do it without her."

"You still together?"

"She passed a few years back. Cancer."

"Sorry, bro." Wesley handed over the stainless mess forks for Levon to dry. "So, who's helping you through shit?"

"Now? My girls. Have to stay on the narrow path for them." Levon dropped the forks onto the pile of mess ware. "Before that, it was Xanax washed down with Maker's Mark."

"I was on all that shit before I come up here. I decided my problem was me, and why should I be inflictin' myself on everyone I gave a shit for? Once I come up here, I felt better after a while. Not having to deal with it. Not having to talk to folks."

"Still wake up screaming?" Levon asked, but he was smiling.

"Sometimes, yeah." Wesley lowered his head and grinned.

"You can't ever un-see the shit we've seen."

"Can't un-feel it neither."

14

The investigation was being pursued in two parts now.

Vince Holland took on the hunt for Oscar Cruz's cousin Richie, who turned out to be Enrique Damian Cruz, an ex-con with a thick file of priors going back ten years and two active county warrants for failure to appear in court on Class III felony possession. He did indeed have a pair of black teardrops inked under his left eye and bore a passing resemblance to the actor who played Ant-Man's friend.

Richie Cruz swore he didn't know anyone named Angel. He was lying big time. In truth, he knew so many scumbags named Angel that it took sorting through prints taken from the Cruz Coachman to make a match. Tomas "Angelito" Suarez was arrested coming out of an ABC in Westlawn and was eager to hand over both Cruz cousins in exchange for "a little understanding, you know?"

He had no idea that Oscar Cruz was dead and was dismayed to learn Richie was already in custody. He sweetened his offer by telling them about two brothers he knew who were up to their asses in *niños y niñas*, selling and buying kids like commodities. They had an apartment over in Darwin Downs. Beto and Angel—yet *another* Angel—Villamonte.

Laura Strand's path to the truth took her deep into the hell of the foster care system of Madison County with juvenile advocate Betsy Ritter as her chain-smoking Virgil.

All three children were indeed registered in the foster care system, and as Nadine had detailed, they were passed around from one foster home to another. Often, they were placed less than a year in any one home before being moved again. Nadine had been in care from the age of five when her parents died in a house fire. The eleven-year-old boy they had taken from the Coachman was Antony Contrera. He was in his eighth year in the system after his mother had been sentenced to ten years at Tutwiler for a variety of charges involving narcotics. In the third year of her sentence, she'd died of an overdose in the prison infirmary. The youngest, Lacey May Brees, had been found when she was an infant in an abandoned car in the lot of a Super Walmart.

"I don't want to tell you how to do your job," Betsy told Laura over breakfast at a Perkins.

"Well then, why don't you tell me how you do *your* job?" Laura dabbed grease off her turkey bacon strips and white egg scramble with the corner of a napkin. She wondered how the woman seated across from her maintained her bantam weight, given the cheese omelet, hash browns, and biscuits and cream gravy Betsy was wolfing down.

"First thing you have to know is that everyone you talk to will be looking to cover their ass. The social workers, their supervisors, and the foster parents. The system isn't broken like I said before. It's on fire. Too many kids and not enough foster parents or volunteers.

It's an environment built for abuse, and the only thing there's no shortage of is bottom feeders coming in to take advantage."

"Why aren't more kids adopted?" Laura said. "These kids were all young when they were orphaned. It seems like they'd be prime candidates."

"Because most folks can't afford the fees involved with legal adoption. The lawyers and the courts made sure of that. And the hoops you need to jump through to qualify keep a lot of parents out of the mix."

"Aren't there qualifications for taking in foster kids?"

"There are—on paper. But the system's so overloaded that those rules get worked around. I've seen foster parents who can't take care of themselves caring for five or six kids in their house."

"Why do they do it?"

"For the county checks. There's a lot of benefits offered for taking kids in."

"Is there anyone taking kids just because they want to offer them a home?"

"Sure. Most foster parents do it for the right reasons. But there's enough bad apples out there to keep me as busy as a one-legged man in a shin-kicking contest."

"Then how do I approach this? I have the foster homes these kids were last assigned to and the records from the juvenile court. Each one of these kids is technically still in the care of their assigned home. Our best guess, from Nadine and Antony's information, is that Oscar Cruz took illegal custody of them six to seven months ago and Lacey May somewhere near the end of summer."

Betsy chewed a mouthful of omelet, waving her empty fork to let Laura know she was working on something.

"I'd let the county bust them," she said after a long

pull of black coffee. "The kids are absent, whereabouts unknown. That's reckless endangerment and criminal neglect. More than enough to hold them for you until you get some answers."

"I'm not even sure what questions to ask."

"You need to look into their care histories and press them on every inconsistency. If they sold kids off once, it figures they've done it before. This kind of shit goes round and round."

"With the help of a federal judge, I can make RICO stand up here."

"That's your business," Betsy said. "But County should pick them up."

"We let County make the collars, but the marshals should have a presence at the raids."

"No raids. These houses have at-risk kids in them. You don't want to put them through that." Betsy waggled her fork over her plate. "You make these sumbitches come to you."

"How does that work exactly?"

"Send the fosters letters telling them there's a problem with their next monthly check. In the letter, you assign them all an appointment at the county court-house. Bust them there."

"You have a devious mind, Betsy," Laura said.

"Whatever gets the job done," Betsy said and dabbed up the last of the cream gravy with a bit of biscuit.

15

Justin Hicks had two offices in the Huntsville area. One was a two-room office suite near the county courthouse. The other was in a professional park in Brookhurst.

The county seat office was problematic—too much law enforcement presence. The Family and Children offices in an annex to the courthouse were where the lawyer did most of his business. It was an armed camp with metal detectors and deputies at every entrance, and for good reason. This was the home of Domestic Relations, where divorced couples went to deal with issues such as alimony, child support, and custody. Tempers were high, and often what began as a negotiation, with one wrong word could turn into a fistfight or worse.

Levon had his own experiences in that building after Arlene passed away and his in-laws tried to take away his visitation rights with Merry. He'd been angry in his time and with good cause, but he'd never felt the kind of white-hot rage that filled him when dealing with the intractable staff who decided who was fit and who was not to see their own child. Every time he read or heard about a shooting incident at a courthouse somewhere, he imagined it took place when some dad finally lost control over a custody order keeping him from his children. More times than not, Levon was right.

The office park in Brookhurst was a labyrinth of twenty or more single-story office buildings. The Home and Heart adoption agency was situated near the end of a cul-de-sac between an allergist and a title company.

Levon pulled into a space in front of the allergist, where he could look like he was waiting for a patient inside. He had a good view of the front of Home and Heart. It was after lunch and business was brisk at the allergist's, forcing Levon to take up a more removed position in front of an empty unit with FOR LEASE signs in its windows.

Home and Heart wasn't busy at all. Two spaces were occupied by the same cars throughout the day: a pewter Mercedes sedan with a vanity plate that read KIDS 1 and an older model Kia. Levon assumed the Mercedes belonged to Hicks. The import would be for his secretary or receptionist.

Throughout the afternoon, a few cars came and went, package deliveries and a couple of cars parked long enough for appointments. It was getting dark when the allergist and home title place shut down and locked up. The lights stayed on at Home and Heart. At ten minutes to six, a woman wearing a puffy down parka over a pants suit exited the building, got into the Kia, and drove off. She didn't lock the doors on her way out, meaning the place was still open and Justin Hicks was alone inside.

Levon gave it a few minutes, then opened the door to step from the truck. An Escalade pulled up in front of Home and Heart. Levon drew back into the cab. A large man in a leather coat emerged from the Escalade and went inside the office, leaving the engine running and headlights on. He was a broad-shouldered black man wearing a gray cloth cap pulled low over his eyes. He moved with the assurance of someone who was familiar with this office.

Less than two minutes passed before the doors opened and a different man exited, a beefy white guy just as tall as the black man who'd entered but with a good fifty or more pounds on him. It wasn't Hicks. This man moved as if his knees were giving him trouble. He wore a wool jacket trimmed in leather in some school's colors. His head was bare, dark hair receding, and a bushy mustache drooped to a double chin. The heavier man got in the Escalade, circled around the cul-de-sac, pulled past Levon, and took off.

Fifteen or more minutes passed, and the lights inside Home and Heart went out. Justin Hicks exited, followed by the black man in leather. Hicks wore a dark raincoat open over a business suit, with a white silk scarf draped around his neck. He locked up while the black man made for the Mercedes and slid his bulk behind the wheel. Tossing a leather briefcase in ahead of him, Hicks got in the rear seat.

The Mercedes pulled away. Levon gave it time to get out of sight around a curve before starting his truck to follow.

———

LEVON FOLLOWED the Mercedes at a discreet distance on the forty-minute drive south to the Owens Cross Roads section of Huntsville. It was an easy tail in heavy traffic that finally thinned out on Hobbs Island Road. The Mercedes pulled onto a private road that cut through a gap in the thick tree line along the road. Levon hung back.

After taking his time making a left against traffic to

give his prey a lead, he made the private road and gunned the Avalanche. At his first glimpse of red tail-lights through the trees, he cut his headlights to follow the winding one-lane road through the dark woods.

The Mercedes came to a stop on the apron of a drive-way. Levon stopped at the start of a bend in the road. The sedan puffed blue exhaust while waiting for a wrought iron gate set between two fieldstone uprights to open. Levon eased the Avalanche forward and watched the red lights roll down a crushed stone driveway shoul-dered by tall pines. The lights vanished around a turn. Seconds later, lights gleamed through the trees from a source at the end of the driveway. Motion detector lights, most probably. That would probably mean cameras too.

Levon followed the road to where it ended at a gated entrance to another property. He turned around and headed back north.

———

RATHER THAN WAIT until morning for a public library to open, Levon parked the Avalanche on the rear lot of a Westin and entered the hotel through a side door that opened onto a hallway lined with conference rooms. He took a seat in the lobby out of sight of the clerk at the registration desk but with a view of the business center. Through the glass walls of the center, he could see only one guest inside, a guy about his age in slacks and a dress shirt, seated at one of three public computer terminals. His suit jacket was draped over the back of the chair. The guy was moving the mouse and scrolling but not touching the keyboard, probably checking emails or social media posts. End of the business day, he wasn't typing any responses.

When the guy stood to take his jacket off the seat-back, Levon crossed the lobby to the business center. The guy slid an arm into his jacket, giving Levon a curt nod. Levon nodded back and took a seat at the nearest terminal. Once the guy left, Levon switched seats to sit at the screen the guy had vacated.

The guy was still logged on. Most people forgot to sign off from their sessions on public terminals. They were used to open access at work and home and on mobile devices. Levon had counted on that.

He went to realtor.com and typed in the address of the Hicks home in Owens Cross Roads. The house was not currently for sale but was still included in the multi-listings on the site from past sales. A gallery of photos showed up on the screen from when the house had been on the market eight years ago. The main house was eight thousand square feet, with a detached four-car garage, a pool house, and a guest suite on five wooded acres. Faux antebellum style with a caged-in pool and hot tub that would never be found at Tara. An aerial shot showed houses in a similar price range on lots of no less than five acres bordering the Hicks home to the north, south, and west.

Current listings had one of these properties on the market. From the photos, it appeared to be staged for sale but unoccupied. It might serve as a surveillance post. He'd need to watch the house for a day or so to get an idea of the rhythms and patterns: how many lived there, and when were they at home or away.

"You come up with a name for that hound yet?" Jessie Hamer asked as she climbed out of her truck.

Fern Cade was walking away from the stable, pushing a barrow heaped with manure, a Jack Russell bounding before him and a rangy bluetick hound loping alongside. Both dogs made for Jessie.

"I left that up to the girls, and they were a while sorting it out," Fern told her. He took the load to the foot of a steaming mound in a three-sided cinder-block enclosure at the edge of the broad farmyard.

"Option paralysis," Jessie said, approaching. Rascal, the Jack Russell, leapt high in the air to beg for her attention. The hound, tongue lolling, followed Fern.

"Muleheaded, more like it." He tipped the barrow to empty it. "The girls are mucking the stalls if you need to talk to them."

"I wanted to see Levon, but I see his truck is gone."

"He's been keeping himself busy. Late nights and gone most days."

"I know you have to put the hours in when you're

building a business." Jessie ran her own large animal practice, Riverstone Veterinary.

"Been mostly Merry helping me with that," Fern said, setting the barrow down. "Levon cosigned my loan and went to the closure on the garage building. Whatever he's doin', it's his own business. He keeping it from you, too?"

"I've barely seen him. We talked on the phone a few nights back. He sounded tired."

"You know he cares for you, Jessie."

"In his way. Though it's not hard to see where Merry gets her mule-headedness."

"Hopey's not much better. Hell, you'd think she *was* a Cade. Come on in the house, and we can talk there."

Jessie took a seat in the kitchen while Fern poured them both mugs of coffee from the percolator. Fern made cowboy coffee, as thick as soup. She asked him to run a bit of water in hers, then flavored it with honey and milk until it was potable. The bluetick settled into a dog bed in a corner of the room while Rascal kept circling the table, nails clicking on the tiles.

"So, what name did they decide on?" Jessie asked after her first tentative sip.

"Bella," Fern said, setting a plate of cookies on the vinyl tablecloth before taking a seat.

The hound's ears perked up at the mention of her name, mouth dropping open in a sloppy grin.

"Suits her," Jessie said.

"You know, Merry might know more of what her dad is up to than I do. I've been tied up with paperwork for the still."

"I don't want to do that. I used to have a maiden aunt when I was a kid. She'd pester me with questions about how my parents were getting along every time she'd get me alone. Super-creepy."

"Well, all's I can say is that he started the late nights after all that business with Teddy Lee. Spends a lot of time in his work shed with the door bolted. Reminds of how he was the time he came home after his first deployment."

"I'm the one sewed up his cousin's gunshot wound. You'd think after doing a favor like that, a girl'd earn something like an explanation. All Levon would say was I was better off not knowing."

"He's most probably right, you know."

"Yeah. Yeah. Sure. The less I know, the less I can testify to."

Fern reached across the table to touch her hand.

"Now, you know it's more than that. He turned to you when he had no other choice. It was about family. He only wants to make sure that whatever it was Teddy Lee and him were up to will never touch you and your little girl."

"He's never going to settle down, is he? He's always going to be like this. Driven to act." Jessie drummed her fingers on the mug.

"Levon's not much different than these dogs here." Fern nodded at Rascal, who had finally come to rest at Jessie's feet. "They like having a job guarding a flock or hunting game. Without it, they get restless. Mean, even. Levon has to have a purpose. He finds peace in doing. Even as a kid, he was like that, only he used that energy for hellraising back then. Joining the Corps gave him a direction for all that, but all that bad shit he saw didn't blunt his edge; it sharpened it. The man can't find peace in his mind."

"Sounds more like a shark than a dog. He has to keep moving or die. My first husband was in the service. I saw a change in him after he came back from his first deployment in Iraq. But he was still the same man." Gary

Hamer, an Army Ranger, had been killed in the Helmond on what was supposed to be his final deployment to Afghanistan.

"Depends on who a man is going in, I guess." Fern shrugged. "Some it makes worse, some it makes better, and some come out the same way they went in."

"Where does Levon fit in that equation?"

"In the Corps, we called it 'born again hard.' Whatever my nephew went through, it's set him on a path he can't find his way off of."

"Or doesn't want to."

"Could be a whole lot worse. Could be pills or drink. I seen both. Hell, I *done* both when I got home. Levon wrestled with that some too till he met up with Arlene. Marrying her and having Merry brought him out of himself some. Then he was called up again. He come back when Arlene got diagnosed. Now he lives for his little girl. Little *girls*, now."

"By staying away and up all hours by himself?"

"He's dealing with something. It'll end."

"You said he cares for me," Jessie said. "You know I care for him."

"I know that. You see yourself keeping with him, or maybe you're thinkin' about moving on?"

"I can't. I thought about *all* that, and I can't." She turned away from him, wincing. "Shit, that's strong coffee."

He half-rose from his chair when she pushed away from the table to make for the door.

"Tell him I was by," she said.

His promise to do so was cut off by the slamming door. Her truck sprayed gravel as she turned it around to tear down the long driveway toward the road.

17

With varying degrees of difficulty, the twin set of busts were successful.

Strictly as an observer, Laura accompanied the county sheriffs to the lobby of the courthouse annex. The foster parents of Nadine, Antony, and Lacey May were braced while they were signing in at the security desk for morning appointments scheduled thirty minutes apart. Each person went quietly, placing their hands on their heads and one wrist at a time at the small of their backs for cuffing with the casual ease of repeat offenders. The first pairs of arrestees were placed in a breakroom out of sight of the lobby until the last was taken. All were frog-marched to the county sheriff's office, where their warrants were turned over, and each was booked on charges of human trafficking and child endangerment. They were taken in a van to the county lockup to await arraignment the following morning.

Deputies accompanied officers from Family and Children to the three foster homes to round up any adults on the premises and to remove any kids to county custody. All this was done before the first three in lockup were allowed near a phone to give warning. Four adults, three spouses of the arrestees, and a guy who claimed to be a live-in uncle were arrested. Eight children were taken from the homes. Again, easy-peasy, the prey caught napping and unawares.

Not so the arrests of *los hermanos* Villamonte.

As US Marshal Vince Holland put it:

"Textbook entry, right? We knock the door down in this shithole apartment complex and we're in. This crib is nas-*tee*. Trash everywhere and smells like ass. It's a shotgun two-bedroom, and there's the six of us sweeping the corners. First thing we run into is this fucking dog, a mastiff crossed with the rottweiler and a crocodile. It launches, I mean *launches* off a sofa right for Bo Charles. Two of us tase this fucker, and it goes down twitching.

"Then Spaz is yelling from a bedroom. He's yelling, 'Stop, motherfucker! Stop!' But this asshole, Angel, is out of bed and runs right through the glass of a sliding door onto a balcony. Goes through that glass like Mick Jagger and over the rail, only he don't *fly* like an angel and lands on top of a Sierra.

"Mountain and Rizzo are down there waiting for him, and I don't know what kind of shit this guy was on; he puts up a fight. After falling flat on his ass three stories! Little wiry bastard weighs maybe one-ten with his clothes on. Still, it takes Mountain and Rizzo both to get him down and chewing grass. Mountain says it's the best workout he's had in weeks. Colder than hell and both of them sweatin' bullets. The little perp is all fucked up, but Rizzo still has to bitch-slap him to get him to stop spitting on the seats in the back of their unit."

"And Beto?" Laura asked.

"Oh, it gets better. I take lead on bedroom two, and big brother is nowhere to be found. We know he's home because we're up on their phones and heard him talking to his mom just before we took the door. 'Hey, Moms, me and Angel's jus' hangin'' and 'Yeah, I know it's *abuela's* birthday tomorrow.' And shit like that. But no Beto. Not in the bathroom or their Roach Motel kitchen or either bedroom. That leaves the closets, right? I'm moving on the closet in bedroom two, making all the dire threats to what could be just dirty laundry and a sneaker collection. Me and Bo Charles and Tolly are guns up on the folding doors when Beto explodes out of the closet, and guess what he has in his hands?"

"No idea," Laura said.

"A samurai sword. A fucking *samurai* sword like he's gonna go Uma Thurman on us. And his eyes are like pinwheels, spinnin'. He's fucked up on the same shit that turned his buddy Angel into a tiger. Turns out the sword is just some piece of shit he got off eBay, and Bo Charles has it off him after two swings. Then it's elbows and boots until the three of us can get him on the carpet. We have him double-cuffed, and he keeps kicking at us. We had to tie his legs with strips of a bedsheet. He looked like a mummy from the waist down by the time we got him secured. Tolly was all for tossing him off the balcony after his pal. Like he'd ever remember us doing it. But you know how it is; every asshole has a cellphone, and *every* asshole with a cell phone was outside and in the hall playing Geraldo."

"Where are they now?" Laura asked.

"The hospital, Decatur-Morgan, until they come down. You can probably talk to them in the morning."

"Bright side? They're probably too out of it to ask for legal counsel."

"Fucked up as *they* are? They'd be asking for the *Jedi* council. I'll head over later and read 'em their rights once the shit starts wearing off."

"You want to be there for the Q&A?"

"Oh, yes, Strand. I want to *hear* these assholes' version of how the bust went."

————

THE LAST THING NORBETO "BETO" Villamonte could remember was buying beer at a Racetrac on Tuesday afternoon, and here it was Thursday morning.

He sat at a steel table in the Madison County Annex Detention Facility with his wrists cuffed through a metal ring welded to the tabletop. Opposite him sat a little black bitch in a US Marshals windbreaker and Harry Potter glasses. Some big surfer-looking fucker leaned against the far wall, eye-fucking him.

His head hurt. His legs hurt. His neck hurt. His arms and his ass hurt. He had two broken fingers on his left hand wrapped together in a splint. There was a gap in his lower teeth that felt fresh, the gums raw where the roots had come out. The shit was mostly out of his system, and he could feel a chill coming on even as sweat rolled down his back to his ass crack under the yellow county jumpsuit.

"Your rights were read to you, and you've been charged with breaking federal laws related to trafficking and child exploitation," the little *puta* said, a notepad by her hand.

"I want a lawyer."

"We'll let you know when he gets here."

"Fuck you till that happens."

"You're going to get a bail hearing, and it doesn't look good. You need to encrypt your devices better. Or not at all. '123456' is not a strong password, Mr. Villamonte."

"That shit ain't legal. Looking in a man's computer and shit."

"You *do* need a lawyer, shithead." This from the surfer-looking fucker.

"Our warrants are very specific, Mr. Villamonte," the *puta* continued on. "We have all your contacts, browsing history, and text messages."

"That don't mean shit."

"It does mean shit, Mr. Villamonte. It means very *bad* shit for you." The *puta* leaned forward to eye-fuck him through her round lenses. "We're going to request no bail for you, and I'm guessing the federal judge you'll be seeing will go along with that request."

"Doin' time ain't nothing."

"This is federal time, Mr. Villamonte. Big Sandy. Beaumont. Marion," she went on. "Are you familiar with them? Have you heard of them?"

Beto had heard of them and nothing good. Baby-rapers served hard time in places like that, locked up in isolation till they banged their skulls open on the walls or buttfucked with plunger handles until they bled out in the showers. A far cry and a world away from the minimum security lock-ups he'd done time in.

"Or you could help us out." The *puta* sat back. "We could drop charges and let the county have you."

"You spend a few years on a farm workin' weights, gettin' your pump on," the surfer added.

He knew they were gaming him, but that didn't make it not so. If they had his devices, then they had him by the *cajones*. His whole fucking life was on that phone and laptop, a roadmap to the dark side of his soul. Thousands of pictures of him with young flesh. All his clients and all the sites he'd visited with more images and video.

"We have Angel too," the *puta* said. "He's in the next room, and we're gonna offer him what we're offering you."

"And the first one takes it gets a ticket to a county farm," the surfer put in.

"I got a lawyer you need to see," Beto said and watched them beetle their brows, eye-fucking him again.

The *puta* scooped up her pad and made to stand up. The surfer pushed off the wall, chin raised in mock pity.

"No! No! It ain't that way!" Beto pulled at his cuffs, running the chain through the ring with a rasping sound. "Not *my* lawyer. *Another* lawyer."

"What are you talking about?" The *puta* took her seat, interested once more.

"This white guy. He's a lawyer. He sets up the buys."

18

The scent of grilling deer steaks filled the holler. Fat dripped off the meat on the spit to hiss in the open fire. Potatoes and frozen corn ears wrapped in foil were buried in the embers to bake.

Levon and Wesley Ruskin stood watching the fire, taking pulls from cold Heinekens Levon had humped over the ridge in a cooler.

"I like mine bloody," Wesley said, placing his empty in the cooler and snagging a fresh one.

"That's fine at a steakhouse." Levon nodded. "But I prefer my game meat cooked through."

"You worried about worms?"

"Aren't you?"

"Deer parasites don't affect humans. Read that somewhere. 'Sides, if this buck had bad worms, it woulda' died when the cold weather hit."

"I guess. I'll stay with well-done anyway."

They ate the steaks, potatoes, and sweet corn, liberally sprinkled with the hot sauce Levon had brought along. Together they cleaned the plates and mess ware at the spring head before returning to the fire to share the last of the six-pack. The sun was behind the ridge now. Deep shadows descended through the trees as the sky turned gray.

After a long silence, Levon said, "You know, there's better hollers than this one."

"Better how?" Wesley pried the cap off a Heinie and took a seat on the cooler.

"I know one where you can have a roof over your head, at least."

"Those tend to have people in them."

"Not this one. 'Sides, you're gonna have to come back to the world sometime."

"Who says?"

"The American Dental Association. And doesn't that leg of yours need maintenance now and then?"

"I been holding out on that." Wesley unconsciously rubbed at his left leg above the prosthetic.

"You can come with me today up to my truck." Levon shrugged. "I'll take you over to the place. There's a propane stove and an outhouse. A clean water spring runs down the middle of it, and it's loaded with game. No one's hunted there for a long while. There's even a shower."

"I get the hint." Wesley lowered his eyes and grinned.

"Wouldn't hurt."

"What about the people who own it?"

"They moved on a long while back."

Wesley studied the fire for a while before turning to Levon.

"Why you trying to get me to move?"

"You can't live back up in here forever. Think of it as a baby step. And this way, I don't have to hump up and down the ridge anymore."

"It all wooded like this?" Wesley nodded at the trees hemming in the narrow clearing he called home.

"Some wooded. Mostly open ground. You can see people coming a mile off."

"What'll I do there that's different from here?"

"I might just have a job for you."

"You gonna be my boss now?"

Levon shrugged. "More like partners. Strictly free-lance. Offer stands even if your lazy ass doesn't want the job."

"Man, I do miss a cold beer now and then," Wesley said, examining the empty in his hand.

———

THE FOLLOWING morning Levon drove Wesley to his new home.

"This place have a name?" Wesley watched the trees go by from the passenger seat of the Avalanche.

"Sugar Run. After the spring runnin' through it," Levon said, piloting up the rutted road that ran through pines that brushed the sides of the truck.

"How you know this place?"

"Everyone in the county knows this place."

"It's famous for somethin'?"

"Something like that."

When the Avalanche broke out of the trees, the ground leveled off. Wesley could see rusted metal rooftops in the middle of a field of scrub brush that had turned brown in the cold air. As they got closer, he could see a double-wide and a dog run with a shed inside. There was some kind of open pavilion like picnickers used at state parks. Hanging from the ceiling of the pavilion over the picnic benches was a faded flag, a Nazi banner with a black swastika in a white circle against a field of red turned pink over time.

"What'd you say this place was famous for?" Wesley asked.

"It used to belong to the local Klan klavan."

"*Used* to? Who run 'em off?'

"I persuaded the last two holdouts to find another place to hang out."

"Shit," Wesley said when he spied the cardboard targets faded yellow where they were stapled to posts at the end of a target range. Caricatures of scowling black men with big lips and yard-wide Afros peppered with holes from bullets and shot.

"Yeah, you want to tidy up while you're here," Levon said.

"You sure this place is vacated?"

"I figured, if the original tenants came back, you could tell them the place was under new management."

Levon pulled up to the double-wide and helped Wesley unload the goods from the rear of the truck: his rifle, rucksack, waterproof locker, and what remained of the deer carcass wrapped in burlap. They carried the goods inside the shadowy interior of the double-wide that had served as the meeting hall for the local chapter since the height of its membership just before World War II.

The open room featured long tables and folding chairs, standing and collapsed, now scattered across the leaf-strewn floor. A platform at the end of the room supported a wooden pulpit with a microphone stand attached. Behind that hung a banner, a mockery of the American flag with a cross in place of the stars and, at the center of the cross, a diamond shape that contained a stylized single drop of blood. The Stars and Bars, a ten-foot Confederate battle flag, hung from one wall. A neighborhood watch poster was yellowing on another wall. It featured a hooded

Klansman holding an outsized sword with the promise that the Klan was keeping watch. Another wall featured a row of framed pictures of cross burnings and meetings and one photo of unhooded men in Klan robes handing out sandwiches and lemonade to children. Judging from the clothing the kids wore, it was from the 1950s.

There was a kitchen area and a pair of rooms off to one side with boxes stacked against the walls.

"Like I said, the stove is still hooked up to propane. So's the fridge, but you'll probably want to give them both a good scrubbing," Levon said.

"There any gas left in the tank?"

"Probably not. I'm gonna make a run to Sam's Club when I leave here and pick up some new tanks," Levon said. "You wanna come along?"

"Naw."

"Not ready for that?"

"I'd rather stay back here and get settled in." Wesley leaned in the door to inspect the kitchen. "Fifty years of bacon grease all over everything in here."

"The place is well-seasoned. I'll bring back cleaning supplies, along with other stuff you'll need. Anything else you want?" Levon said on his way to the door.

"I'd murder someone for a Big Mac and fries," Wesley called. "Make it two."

19

Two of the sets of foster parents folded early in their interrogations.

Laura Strand was lead on this task force, but she knew her strengths and weaknesses. Formerly with the IRS, she was all about the numbers. She could see patterns, hear lies, and smell malfeasance. But for the kind of work the marshals did, she needed muscle. That was why she requested Vince Holland for the team, a former Army Ranger who'd served in Afghanistan and a doorbuster for the ATF before transferring to the marshals to look for missing kids instead of stolen explosives and guns.

On the game theory side, she knew she'd need some hard-nosed chess players, so she requested a member of her former task force be assigned to her.

Tony Marcoon was once a Philadelphia homicide cop who brought his hard-earned talent for distrust of humanity in general to the job of prying the truth out of suspects either by fear, intimidation, or sleight of mind. He was an imposing figure who could get more out of a witness or perpetrator with a prolonged silence than any other ten agents could get with hours of hardball questioning and threats. Laura was grateful he was willing to postpone his retirement plans a few months to join her in the MCU.

His skills as an interrogator were a joy to watch. She did so from the observation room, where Vince joined her with cold Cokes from the breakroom for both of them. Through the glass, they watched Tony work on his fourth foster parent.

He sat with his back to the glass, and he and the suspect shared Tony's cigarettes despite the NO SMOKING plaque on the wall. The suspect was a white guy in his forties, though he looked a decade or more older. The man sported a bad combover and sallow skin and had a pitted complexion that looked like someone had beaten his face with a golf shoe. This was the foster parent charged with Lacey May as a ward.

"You're saying she ran away?" Tony's voice came through the speaker mounted on the wall.

"That's what I reported," the man said.

"To who? Who'd you report that to?"

"To Family and Children. Called the social worker and all."

"What about the police? You call them?"

"Jolanda done that. She was the kid's social worker."

"The police ever come around? They come to the house and ask questions?"

"Naw." The man smeared the butt of his cigarette dead on the steel tabletop and looked at Tony, who nodded that it was okay for him to help himself to another Marlboro. "Nobody come by. Jolanda said they might, but no one ever did."

"You had kids run away on you a few times before." Tony flicked a lighter to flame and held it out for the man to lean over the table to ignite his smoke.

"Kids do that. Least the kind of kids Diane and I get." Diane was his wife. "These kids got troubles. There's only so much me and Diane can do. They run off, and what are we gonna do about it?"

"You get a lot of six-year-olds running away on you, do you?"

"Sure. Troubled kids is troubled kids." He drew a spiral trail of smoke before his face with a casual wave of his hand. "Don't matter the age. They run off lookin' for more trouble, is all."

"I can tell you're a concerned individual," Tony said, his voice devoid of emotion.

Here it comes, thought Laura.

"Oh, yeah. It pains me when they go off like that. It really does. It works at me, you know that? Wondering where they are or what might have happened. Like I said, there's only so much Diane and I can do. But still, them running away like that always leaves me feeling..." The man clasped his hands together on the tabletop as though in prayer, eyes lowered.

"Troubled," Tony said.

"Yeah," the man said, brightening at the prospect of sharing company with an understanding soul.

"You're full of shit." Tony pushed himself away from the table and left the room, slamming the heavy door.

He burst into the observation room, removed the clip holster from his belt, and laid it on the ledge of the two-way.

"You better take this before I shoot him," he growled.

"We have something you might use," Laura said.

"Anything to shorten my time with these assholes." He lit a fresh smoke and nodded at Vince. "You mind?" Vince shrugged in reply, and Tony went on.

"They're stonewalling, every last one of them. Telling me how they have no idea why the kids ran away. All three kids just ran away, and no one gave a shit. If their fucking dog took off, they'd be out on the street stapling handbills to utility poles. But a kid takes off, and it's business as usual. Kids just being kids. Shitbags, each and every one of them."

"We have a name from the baby-rapers," Vince said.

"Yeah?" Tony said.

"An adoption lawyer," Laura added.

"A lawyer, huh?" Tony's mouth twisted into a wolfish leer.

The bad combover folded within seconds of the mention of the lawyer's name, and it went that way throughout the afternoon and evening; each foster couple, as well as the creepy uncle, caved when the lawyer's name was presented to them. Laura and Vince took part in the second round of questioning to draw a clearer picture of how this Heart and Home agency in Huntsville helped foster parents turn their charges into quick cash.

The story they all stuck to was pure fantasy, but their pathetic desire to believe in it was all they had to cling to, to expiate their sins. They explained in detail how this lawyer was helping to game the system to get these kids out of foster care and into the homes of loving parents who wished to adopt them. These were all deserving Christian families that, for one reason or another, were denied legal adoptions on a variety of technicalities. In their own way, by breaking a few state laws, these foster parents were helping poor, orphaned kids find a future for themselves with a family that wanted them. To hear them tell it, they were eligible for sainthood. And the five to eight thousand paid for each kid didn't hurt either.

One of the lawyers' associates, always a well-dressed, attractive young lady, would pick up the child. From the descriptions, it was probably never the same woman twice. That's when the agreed-upon payment was made in cash. All the foster parents needed to do was wait forty-eight hours, then report the runaway to the kid's assigned social worker. The name and a picture of the kid went into a registry, and that was the end of that.

Like Combover said, "What are we gonna do about it?"

When confronted with the truth of what had happened to the kids, the foster parents' reactions were like capsule psychological profiles. Two of the couples fell immediately into a blame game, with one turning into a serious fistfight. Vince pried them apart and took a sharp elbow in the eye from the wildcat of a wife, who equaled him in weight if not muscle. The third couple opted for denial followed by anger, shouting accusations of entrapment, wrongful arrest, and other terms they'd picked up off TV crime shows.

The creepy uncle just broke down crying. Turned out he didn't know anything about money being paid for kids and felt cheated. He was creepy but not in on the take.

All three couples and the uncle were remanded to county deputies to be charged with child abandonment and a variety of other offenses tied to violations of their agreements to be a part of the foster care program. Tony volunteered to appear at their arraignments in the morning to express the federal government's fond desire that all seven of these losers be held without bail. The last thing anyone needed was the Home and Heart agency getting wind of the arrests.

Laura met Vince in the hotel lobby after a long, hot, stinging shower. Vince had a bag of ice that a girl at the registration desk had gotten for him. He held it to his swollen eye.

"Where do you want to eat?" he asked. "My treat."

"There's a Pizza Hut across the lot from here." She sighed. "It's fast and easy. I have to get back here and write up the warrant for the Hicks son of a bitch. I'll be up half the night."

"What district is this? Eleven?" They crossed the parking lot to the familiar red-roofed restaurant. The smell of garlic, yeast, and onions wafted from the kitchen vents.

"Yeah. That means flying down to Montgomery first thing in the morning. Judge Pickering. I hope to get lucky."

"Not much sleep for you, and it's been a long day."

"At this point, Vince? I'm running on rage," she said, nodding her thanks when he held the door for her to enter the embracing warmth of the pizzeria.

20

He rolled up to the house with the headlights off. The fresh dusting of snow reflected the muted moonlight coming through the silvery clouds that hung low over the pine tops.

The house was a rambling single-story structure in a Spanish revival style that looked out of place in the dense evergreen woods surrounding it, especially with the icing of snow on the ground and the pine boughs. It had sand-colored stucco, an orange tile roof, and a three-car garage off to one side of a circular brick driveway. It was set well back from Hastings Drive, which ran behind Belvedere Road, where the Justin Hicks' house sat.

The front lot of the house was covered in pea gravel in place of the usual shrubbery. This allowed Levon to pull his Avalanche behind the garage and out of sight of the road without leaving any tracks. He stepped out of the truck, pulled a twelve-gauge pump-action from the concealed rack behind the back seat, shouldered a lightly loaded rucksack, and moved into the trees.

A manmade trail of packed cedar chips followed a curtain wall that enclosed the backyard pool area. Levon followed this to find it led into the woods that grew densely behind the property, a common walking or jogging trail that wound through the entire subdivision. It was one of the selling points for this house in the realtor's listing.

The trail branched in the trees and ran behind all the other homes nestled along the curving lanes to either side. It was well after midnight, and most of the homes were dark except for a few outdoor lights. He moved through the trees. They'd all have motion detector lights, and he'd need to be wary of them. Lights would go on, and dogs would bark.

He approached the Hicks house, stopping while still inside the tree line to scan the place first with the naked eye and again with a night-vision lens. There were lights with motion-detection scanners mounted at two corners to cover the caged-in pool area and the broad backyard. The house was dark except for a single low-watt bulb over a rear door. The nascent glow at the front of the house came from solar-powered lamps set in the decorative landscaping. Their light was waning as their batteries went dead.

The trees grew closest to the house along its eastern elevation. Levon took up a post there and laid out a folded groundsheet to kneel on. The lowest branches of a tall spruce provided cover but allowed him a full range of view of the front of the house. The NODs scope revealed another motion detector light mounted under the eaves to cover the area across the front of the house and another at a corner of the garage. An undetected nighttime approach from any direction would be impossible, though the inhabitants of the house would be used to deer setting off the lights with some frequency.

The Mercedes and the Escalade he'd seen out front of Heart and Home were parked on the roundabout driveway at the foot of the stairs leading to the columned veranda that ran across the front of the house. That might mean both bodyguards were at home. It also meant the bodyguards were possibly live-in employees. Hicks was either a very cautious man, or he had competitors that played rough. Or, like a lot of lawyers, Hicks had a long list of people he'd pissed off.

What he could see of the house told Levon very little other than it was well-secured. There were no stickers or signs for security companies in the yard or on the house. That meant nothing. Hicks might have decided not to display whatever firm was responsible for watching over the house.

Everything was added up to a big fat zero for any kind of nighttime incursion. There were too many things he didn't know concerning what went on inside the house and what he might face there to plan a break-in. Thanks to the real estate sites, he had access to the full floor plan and had been able to take a virtual video tour through the entire house. Helpful, but only a start.

His best opportunity might be in the daytime. He'd eliminated the idea of taking Hicks either at his office or en route. Sure, it cut the bodyguard force in half, but it meant doing things swiftly, and that was generally messy. It was better to brace Hicks here in an isolated location than in a more public place with loads of eyes-on and the chance of law enforcement showing up.

It would have to be the house. It would have to be early morning.

There was one more thing he could confirm before calling it a night.

Levon rose to his feet to take a step out of the trees to

activate the nearest motion light. He needed to know about dogs.

Just as he broke from cover, he heard a clang and a grinding noise from the other side of the driveway.

The door in front of one of the garages was going up. A light mounted on the opening mechanism revealed the garage to be empty. Tires crunching on macadam came from the direction of the road. Headlights flashed through the trees. Someone was either visiting or coming home. Considering the late hour, it was someone returning home. Levon stepped back into the sheltering dark.

Another Escalade, this one a deep blue, came into view and pulled into the garage. As it did, lights on the front of the house and garage came on, bathing the turn-around in brilliance. Lights shone from the second floor, followed by more light from the glass panels on either side of the double front doors.

A woman exited the garage, stabbing a remote that brought the garage door down. She walked like a younger woman, her long leather coat trimmed in fur swaying open as she moved toward the house. Blonde hair loose under a wool cap. The sound of her booted feet echoed off the fronts of the buildings. A leather purse swung from her hand.

The front doors opened to frame her in a bar of yellow light. Levon focused his lens on the doorway. Hicks stood backlit in sweats or pajamas. He spoke to the approaching woman. Levon couldn't hear the words, but the tone was harsh, scolding. The woman, or girl, shrugged as she climbed the steps to the veranda. Hicks kept up his tirade until she was in the house and the door slammed, cutting off his voice.

The ruckus proved one thing beyond the shadow of a doubt.

Hicks didn't keep dogs.

Levon gathered his gear to hike back through the woods to his truck. He'd be back before dawn to watch the morning routine at the house. He'd look for patterns then, and opportunities.

He had time to do this right.

21

Laura Strand, fueled by rage and black coffee, did indeed stay up most of the night.

She composed a surveillance warrant based on the accusations of Beto Villamonte as independently corroborated by his brother Angel and the foster parents responsible for the kids taken in the trailer park raid.

The warrant called for a twenty-four/seven surveillance on Justin Avery Hicks of 36 Belvedere Road in a Huntsville suburb. It made all the assurances that this request for surveillance was based on the witness testimony of six individuals associated with the subject. All available evidence pointed to Hicks as being a principle in what looked like a criminal conspiracy whose crimes included child abduction, child imprisonment, human trafficking, and sexual abuse of minors. She wanted to add slavery to the list but considered that a bit of a stretch.

What Laura and MCU were looking for was to tap the phone lines at the Hicks residence and the offices of Heart and Home, the adoption agency the lawyer ran. They also stressed the need for eyes-on surveillance, an

around-the-clock tail to wake Hicks up in the morning
and put him to bed at night. Laura herself would do a
deep dive into every adoption arranged through Hicks'
agency as well as any contacts he had with foster homes.
Though Hicks had no criminal record beyond a drunk
and disorderly when he was studying law at Loyola,
there was more than enough shade thrown on him by
two convicted traffickers to justify giving him a long
hard look.

———

"MA'AM, WELCOME TO MONTGOMERY," a voice above
her said.

Laura came awake, blinking up at a smiling face of a
man in a uniform dress shirt with epaulets and gold pips
on his collar. He looked like a crew member on a cruise
ship. For a flashing moment of confusion, she tried to
remember where she was.

The five other passengers on the puddle-jumper
twin-prop were in the aisle, retrieving their carry-ons
from the overheads. The last thing she recalled was
closing her eyes for a second just after takeoff from
Huntsville. She must have crashed for the whole thirty-
minute flight to Montgomery.

A cab ride to the federal building later, Laura was
waiting in the outer office of the 11th District judge who
had agreed to take a look at her warrant request. A clerk
for the judge, a young white man with a fixed smile and a
syrupy Carolina accent, asked her if there was anything
she needed. Coffee? A tea, perhaps? What he was telling
her, in his own way, was that she looked like shit. She'd
seen the evidence herself in a brief stop in the downstairs ladies' room, where she'd made a vain attempt to
straighten her makeup and clothing.

Twenty minutes of struggling not to nod off later, she was shown into the judge's office.

After a painstaking reading of the warrant request and three copies of the warrant form, Judge Leon C. Pickering said, "Well, everything appears to be in order here." He folded his reading glasses and set them in front of the framed portrait of his half-dozen grandchildren that sat on his desk.

Laura noticed he did not pick up his pen.

"We'd like to start immediately with surveillance, Your Honor," she said.

He held a hand up to her in a gentle gesture to ask for her patience. Laura got a sinking feeling.

"I would like to make my own inquiries before signing on to this," the judge said with a simpering smile.

"We have sworn testimony from eight of Hicks' associates that—"

The cautioning hand came up once more.

"I see no cause to allow haste to take precedence over reason here. Surely, a day or so won't make much difference to your case at this point." That simpering smile again.

It would make all the difference, and Pickering damned well knew that, Laura thought. The Villamontes and the foster parents had already been in contact with their lawyers. How long until the word got around that they were in custody? How long until Hicks found out, either through the jungle telegraph or one of his own brothers on the bar? She fought to keep her eyes, red and burning from lack of sleep, from betraying the rage rising in her.

"There *is* some degree of urgency, Your Honor. The subject of the warrant is a flight risk."

"That's still no cause to rush into this."

"Your Honor, the seriousness of the charges—"

The hand came up again, fingers waggling.

"The seriousness of any charge is not just cause under the law." The judge's smile became brittle. "I'll review this request with all the gravity due to it, given the nature of the crime under suspicion, and make a careful and diligent judgment in a timely manner."

Judgespeak for "Nyah, nyah."

"Thank you, Your Honor," Laura said, standing. "I left my contact information with your clerk."

She took a cab to a Doubletree close to the courthouse to wait while the wheels of justice crawled along in their own sweet time.

22

Levon hiked through the woods early the following morning to take up a more distant vantage point than he had only hours before.

The Escalade and the Mercedes were where they had been before.

While he set up his hide, there was no visible activity around the house.

He wore a winter camo coat in stripes of gray and muted white. With the hood up, he was nearly invisible behind a skein of leafless beech branches and pine boughs dappled with snow. He laid out his ground cover to set his shotgun and ruck on, then set up a 30X spotting scope on a tripod to train on the front door and settled down to wait.

A scan of the house's elevations in daylight revealed tiny surveillance cameras mounted under the eaves by the motion scanners. Two were set to provide downward angles of the driveway turnaround and the approach to the house. It was certain there would be another set to cover the entryway to identify visitors or delivery drivers.

The morning cold was turning his earlobes numb, and he pulled the hood tighter around his head. A thermos of black coffee took some of the chill away. He tucked his gloved hands inside his coat to keep his fingers limber.

As the sky turned violet, then streaked with rust, the smell of onions and frying bacon reached him from the house. Someone was up and preparing for the day. The outside lights winked out, and he could see a glow through the shades of one of the upper rooms.

An hour more and the sun had dispelled the gloom. He heard a shouted male voice from inside the house. The front door slammed open and remained open as the woman from the night before stormed out in a long-legged stride, her long coat swinging. The male voice got louder. With one hand, she aimed a remote at the garage. With the other, she offered the house a solitary finger.

Justin Hicks, in dress pants and shirt and stocking feet, stepped onto the veranda, calling after the woman. She never looked back.

"Katherine!" he called, then "Kathie-Beth! I told you I wanted you home today!"

Levon trained his scope on the woman. He had been right in his earlier guess. She was no older than twenty, maybe even a teenager. Her blonde hair was worn in bangs that covered her eyebrows, and her mouth was set in what looked like a permanent pout.

Hicks stumbled down the steps, cursing at the cold bricks beneath his feet. Levon moved the scope to his face, which was turning a deep crimson. His eyes were wild with rage. In the doorway behind him stood one of the bodyguards, the chubby one. The bodyguard was dressed for work in chinos, a flannel shirt, and some brand of automatic in a pancake holster worn on his belt.

The deep blue Escalade backed out of the garage to make a slewing stop on the slush before tearing down the driveway, gravel flying.

"Goddamn it!" Hicks shouted. "God-fucking-damn it!"

The bodyguard said something that made Hicks turn to the house, feet slipping on the rime of ice covering the steps. The bodyguard stepped forward to help him in, and Hicks waved him away angrily. The door slammed closed, and the house was quiet once more.

Forty-five minutes passed, then Hicks exited the house. This time he was fully dressed, and the other, fitter bodyguard was following. Hicks climbed into the back of the Mercedes, and the bodyguard drove away.

Levon weighed his options.

As near as he could tell, the house was down to one occupant. Hicks and one of his men were gone, and the woman was gone for what looked like the day. Levon decided, based on the depth of Hicks' anger and the words he'd called after her as well as her attitude, that she was most probably Hicks' daughter. It looked like a regular occurrence, him giving her orders and her ignoring them. The more he thought about it, the more convinced he was that this was a parent-child thing. Levon wondered for a moment if he had this kind of teenage rebellion coming his way from either Merry or Hope.

He considered a change in plans, an adjustment. He could take down the chubby bodyguard and have the house to himself, then simply wait for Hicks to get home and ambush both Hicks and the other bodyguard. For that plan to work, it would be best to do it closer to the end of the workday. He had no idea what the daily routine was here. Maybe the chubby bodyguard was meant to relieve his partner sometime during the day the way he'd done before. An unexpected hitch in the schedule might put Hicks and his gunman on alert.

There was no movement or sound from the house. The chubby bodyguard was perhaps asleep or otherwise idle. Levon remained in place for another hour and the status remained the same. The house was quiet.

No need to wait out here in the cold until then. He packed up his gear, folded the groundsheet into the ruck, and shouldered the shotgun.

The sound of a door slamming made Levon turn back to the house. The Escalade came to life, lights blinking. Crouched behind cover, he watched the chubby bodyguard exit the house in a hurry. Chubby marched down the steps to the Escalade, keying the locks open as he rushed for the driver's door.

The man was dressed in sweatpants and a hockey jersey. The laces of his untied sneakers flopped as he walked. Chubby was moving fast for some reason.

Making use of all available cover, Levon moved closer to watch. From the edge of the tree line, he could see the Escalade swing around the circle drive, go into reverse, and back up to the foot of the front steps. Chubby exploded from the car, leaving the door open. The engine was still running. The door indicator dinged.

Four or five minutes passed, and Chubby reappeared carrying a heavy equipment bag in either hand. He opened the rear hatch of the SUV and tossed the bags inside. He was breathing heavily, blowing out clouds of vapor.

He was still in sweats, shoes still untied. That told Levon two things. He wasn't ready to leave immediately, and he was unarmed. No one wearing sweats would be strapped. Also, this sudden activity was not anticipated, not planned.

Levon knew what he was looking at.

A bug out.

Something had spooked Hicks, and he was on the run. He'd called home to order his number two man to throw his most important shit together and get it the hell away from the house.

Levon stood to full height to check the load on his shotgun.

23

"A congressman called for you," Lynette said from behind the reception desk when Justin Hicks entered the lobby of his office.

"Which one?" he said, placing his leather briefcase atop the counter.

"I wrote it down here." Lynette searched the fringe of Post-its stuck around the frame of her monitor. "Did y'all bring rock salt? That walk's mighty slippery."

"Seth's salting it now. You get a name?" Hicks was becoming impatient. He had a few congressmen from several states deep in his favor bank.

"He's called before." She ran her nails over the rainbow of notes, eyes searching.

"Jesus, Lynnette."

"Here it is! Phil Barnes!" She sounded like she expected to win a prize. "You want me to put in a call?"

"I'll handle it. Tell Seth to have some coffee and stick around in case I need him. Better yet, have him come in when he gets done salting the walk."

In his office with the door closed, he draped his coat over a guest chair and unlocked a drawer of his desk.

The drawer contained a half-dozen charged, unregistered burner phones. He tapped the number for the Huntsville office of Phillip Barnes, his local congressman, and got a receptionist there who asked him to hold.

Barnes came on the phone. Hicks opened friendly with a question about an upcoming bowl game. The congressman cut him off and Hicks listened intently, the phone clamped to his ear.

Outside, Seth Tyler finished spreading salt crystals on the icy walk. He was from up north originally, Cincinnati. What these hicks called winter, he called t-shirt weather. Everyone on the radio and TV was talking about what a rough winter it was; there was maybe an inch of snow on the ground, and it'd be in the fifties by noon. A few patches of ice, and everyone drove like snails. Now he was salting the steps with the ice already turning to a thin layer of slush. But Lynette would have kittens if a client slipped and fell on their ass.

Speaking of asses, he didn't mind a little bit of extra work because Lynette had a *great* ass. And from what he overheard when she was on the phone with her mother, things weren't so great at home. Seth wouldn't mind stepping in to offer her some comforting words and a drink or two should she and her husband split up.

He returned the empty scoop to the Lowes bucket full of salt and stamped his feet on the mat before stepping into the office.

"Thanks, Seth." Lynette beamed his way as he removed his coat. "I do appreciate that so much."

That warm 'Bama drawl was even sweeter than usual this morning. Either she'd gotten a high hard one last night, or maybe her faggot husband had finally taken off and she was looking for a replacement.

"Anything for you, Lynette." He gave her a wink that turned her cheeks bright.

"Oh, Justin said to go on in." She nodded at the office door. "He has something he might need done."

Seth opened the office door and made for a guest chair to take a seat while the boss made today's duties clear. He stopped short at the sight of the boss's face.

Justin Hicks was listening to someone on one of his burner phones. Whatever he was hearing had drained his face of color.

24

Man, the boss sounded freaked. Some kind of bad shit was raining down. It was right there in Mr. Hicks' voice, the higher tone and urgency. He made Dewey repeat everything, including reading back the combinations to the safes.

Dewey Bascomb hadn't worked this hard since his failed tryout for the Bucs ten years ago. Following the phone call, he'd cleaned out the wall safe behind the armoire in the master bedroom. Two bags full, now in the cargo area of the Escalade. He huffed and puffed down the basement steps to the second safe, a big standing job that rested against the wall of the utility room that held the central air units.

It must be bad shit if the boss was trusting him with these combinations. He keyed in the numbers and turned the wheel to open the big gun safe. Inside were rifles and shotguns standing upright and shelves for handguns and ammo. On other shelves were file folders, CDs, and a large fireproof box with a handle on top.

Dewey loaded the files into a cardboard carton and lifted the heavy firebox. He humped them up the stairs.

His knees were killing him today with the colder weather, and he felt every step.

He'd been putting off knee replacements for years. It was his goddamned knees that had kept him from going pro. At twenty-two years of age, they'd given out on him after three years of high school ball and four years at USF. All the steroids and cortisone in the world couldn't improve his moves for tryout week in Tampa. He was too slow and too late to the play every time. Out on his ass by the third day.

He was past thirty now, with not much to recommend him but his height and weight. He'd met the boss when he was working the door for a bar in Birmingham. Mr. Hicks had hired him away, and he didn't have to stand by a door anymore, dealing with drunks and breaking up fights. Mostly he was there to run light errands and drive for the man. Sometimes he'd have to toss someone around. Then there was that time in Echols Hill. Some asshole owed the boss money, and he and Seth Tyler had gone over to collect. They'd worked the guy over, but the man wouldn't give. When he called Seth a dirty nigger, Seth had lost his shit. They'd wound up tossing the body in the Wheeler Reservoir. Mr. Hicks never got his money, but he never asked any questions about it either.

Now it looked like this job was coming to an end. Mr. Hicks was taking off, maybe for good; that was obvious. Dewey would miss the weekly check he earned as a "security consultant." Mostly he'd miss living in this fine house and the suite in the guest quarters he shared with Seth. It was nicer than any place he'd ever lived. Way nicer than the two-bedroom bungalow in Bartow he'd grown up in. Even nicer than the apartment he'd lived in when he was at college.

The only thing he could hope for was wherever the

boss was going, Mr. Hicks would take him along. Maybe someplace with a beach. He missed the beach. And warmer weather.

He carried the boxes to the Escalade, sweating despite the cold. The boxes went into the back by the equipment bags. He brought the hatch down and turned back to the house to change clothes and drive over to Heart and Home.

That was when he saw the guy standing near the trees. The first thing he noticed about the guy was the shotgun, a pump with an extended magazine like cops had in their cars. Tall guy in a camo-patterned coat with the hood up over a ball cap. The shotgun was up and aimed at Dewey.

"Hands," the guy said and gestured with the barrel.

Dewey held his hands away from his body and weighed his options. He could do what this guy said. He could head back in the house for his piece. He could make for the open car door and drive off. He could rush the guy, but forty feet separated them.

"Down on your knees," the guy said and took a step onto the driveway. Maybe thirty feet now.

Dewey winced. For a fleeting second, chancing a load of buck seemed preferable to kneeling on the hard brick. He hesitated, then crouched with his hands held out before him.

"Knees. Now." The guy was insistent but not shouting, not mad. Just a guy used to people doing what he said. He stepped closer, then came to a stop.

Dewey crouched lower, waving a splayed hand before him, eyes on the man standing at the edge of the driveway holding the unwavering barrel on him. He realized the guy was trying to stay out of view of the surveillance cameras.

The guy was working out his own options, like how

to get to the Escalade without being seen by the cameras. This guy had scoped the place out. He was after the boss; that had to be it. This guy was the reason why Mr. Hicks was going on the run. This guy was the reason Dewey was about to lose his job and have his life turn back to shit.

In his mind, he heard a whistle. He was back on the grass at Raymond James in a three-point stance. His whole life was riding on the next play. Then came the snap.

Dewey launched.

The guy took a step back and fired. A spray of double-ought knocked Dewey sideways, and he lay on the bricks, gasping and flailing. He heard the crunch of the man's boots on rock salt. The snick-snack of the pump working. A shadow fell over him.

I didn't kneel, he thought as thunder filled his ears.

25

Katherine Elizabeth Hicks piloted her Escalade south on Hobbs Island.

The early morning traffic was going the other way into the city. She tapped the wheel and swayed her skinny hips in the seat in time to Cardi B booming around her.

Her father would have gone to the office by now, so it was safe to go back home after a trip through the Starbucks drive-through. The way he'd been riding her ass since after Christmas, she sure didn't want to see him again today. All his bullshit about choosing a college and how he wanted her to go to Loyola like he had. She wanted to go somewhere up north, not some coon-ass school loaded up with the same mouth-breathing hicks she'd grown up around. Someplace she'd never have to hear another Tim McGraw song.

They'd had one hell of a fight that morning. He'd rousted her out of bed to tell her to shake her ass and get to looking at catalogs.

"I want to see you up and moving around before I head to work."

She told him she'd already picked her schools and rolled over to put her back to him.

"Let me guess, you picked out some nigger school where you'll be dumber coming out than when you went in."

It was a common insult to her choice of higher education, though this time, he'd dropped his voice low so Seth wouldn't hear it down in the kitchen.

"Get outta bed!" He slammed her door and stomped down the stairs.

She got up once he was gone and threw on some clothes. He didn't catch sight of her until she was halfway to the door. Too late, Poppy. She was in the garage and G-O-N-E, smiling at his pantomime rage in the rearview mirror, drowned out by the deep bass of her sound system.

Kathie-Beth slowed the Escalade to pull left into the turn lane for Belvedere Road. The car shuddered when a semi blasted by, startling her. She turned back to the oncoming traffic and saw a car approach the intersection from the east. It was Poppy's Escalade.

She squinted through the winter glare on the windshield to see who was driving and if her father was inside. The driver was alone. The shape was wrong for Dewey, and the color was wrong for Seth. The car powered into a right when a gap opened in traffic. As it passed, she caught a glimpse of the man behind the wheel. A white guy, not Dewey. It was no one Kathie-Beth had ever seen before.

A horn honked behind her. Someone had pulled into the turn lane on her bumper. With a hissed curse, she made the turn and forgot about the minor mystery of who was driving Poppy's SUV.

———

LEVON DROVE the Escalade north on Hobbs Island Road until the next right-hand turn took him onto Hastings Drive.

He drove to the house where he'd left the Avalanche, pulled the SUV alongside it, and cut the engine.

It took maybe two minutes to transfer the two gear bags, the cardboard carton, and the heavy fireproof box into the covered bed of his truck. He was tossing the shotgun and his gear bag onto the rear seat when the high, warbling noise came through the trees.

A woman's scream.

From the Hicks house.

26

"You gonna be down there another day?" Vince Holland asked, his breathing heavy on the phone.

"I don't know," Laura Strand said, lying back on the bed in her hotel room while surfing channels on the TV. "What the hell are you doing?"

"Getting a few reps in," Vince said.

"You on a headset?"

"Yeah." His breath came in a whoosh.

She pictured him in the gym back at the hotel they shared, his tanned muscles beaded with sweat, the veins on his arms standing up. Gross. Laura liked her men sleek like swimmers or runners. Besides, those muscle jocks were too into themselves for her taste.

"You off-duty?" she said.

"For another thirty. I'm goin' in after a shower. Not much to do with you hanging fire. Marcoon's at the courthouse, showing the flag at the arraignments."

"I hate this waiting," she hissed, her eyes on the screen where a panel of women was speaking and waving their hands. Laura could tell they were talking over one another even though she had it on mute. They seemed pleased with themselves. She tabbed over to a soccer match from somewhere.

"The hotel have a pool? Go have a swim. Or take a run." That was Vince's answer to everything. Take some reps. Get your pump on.

"I want to be here when the judge's office calls."

"What are the chances he'll call this soon?"

"Poor to shit outta luck."

Vince chuckled on the other end. She heard the clank of metal on metal.

"You think this judge'll fuck us, Strand?"

"I have that feeling. Like Christmas ain't coming."

"So, what do we do?"

She tabbed off the soccer game to a channel with a show she remembered her dad used to watch. Some white dude in a tweed sport coat was getting the daylights beat out of him by a pair of white guys in an alley. They left him scuffed and bleeding from the lip to climb into some '70s gas guzzler and roar away.

"Strand?"

"We have our guy, right? We know right where he is right now." She sat up on the edge of the bed and slipped her feet into her pumps.

"Sure. We get the green light, we pick his ass up."

"Fuck that shit," she said. "You and the guys get on him now. The house and the office. Nothing says we can't keep an eye on this son of a bitch until the paper comes in."

"We can do that. We can sit on him."

"But discretion, Vince. We don't want this guy to rabbit. I want us to fall on him out of a clear blue sky. You hear me?"

"Just a look-see. Like ninjas. You gonna wait there for the judge?"

"He can fax the warrants," she said, clipping her

holstered Sig at the small of her back and throwing on her coat. "I'm getting a rental. See you in four hours."

———

TWO MADISON COUNTY cars showed up at the Hicks residence to find a deep blue Caddy SUV pulled off into the snow at the side of the drive, driver's side door wide open and the car still running. Some kind of heavy beat music pounded from inside to keep time with the open-door alarm.

The front door of the house was wide open too.

What consumed most of their interest was the body lying on the driveway.

It was a large man in a colorful jersey and sweatpants. He had one sneaker on his foot. The other lay ten feet away. His clothing was stained black with blood, and there was a large pool growing dull, freezing in the cold morning air. Multiple punctures in his clothing indicated a charge or two of shot. The now-hollow rind of what had once been his skull indicated something even more final.

"Pumpkin ball," said one deputy.

"Uh-huh," the other said and raised his weapon to approach the front door.

Without an exchange on tactics, the first deputy put his shotgun to his shoulder and made his way along the side of the house to cover the rear where the place backed up on woods.

"We had a call to speak to the woman," the deputy at the door called. "Ma'am, can you hear me? Did you call for the police?"

A keening, gibbering sound came from somewhere deep inside the house.

"Sheriff's deputy, ma'am. Are you in danger?"

More gibbering.

"Can you come out where I can see you, ma'am?"

"Ben?" The voice of the other deputy on his radio.

He tapped the mike on his shoulder. "You see anything, Johnny?"

"I'm looking through the back sliders into the kitchen."

"She there? The woman who called?"

"Yeah. Rabbit-skin coat, looks like. Scared shitless."

"Can you approach her, calm her down?"

A crackle, then silence from his radio. A sudden shriek from inside.

"Johnny, can you approach her?"

"I just tapped on the glass."

"Can you get her to open the door and let you in?"

"Not till she puts down the steak knife she's swingin' around. She looks like she'd go Xena on me if I stepped inside."

27

"Pull all the files with red tabs and shred 'em. Pull the yellow-tab files and box 'em up!" the boss roared when he exploded out of his office.

The phone on Lynette's desk rang, and she reached for it.

"No calls!" He swept the phone from her grasp and sent it tumbling across the lobby.

"Mr. Hicks?"

"Boxes are in the storage room!" He stabbed a finger at the closet and stormed back into his office.

Lynette loaded the paper files into cartons, which Seth carried out to the Mercedes while Mr. Hicks pulled the hard drives from all the CPUs.

"What's happening?" Lynette leaned over a carton to whisper to Seth.

"Ask the boss," he said and lifted the carton to head for the door.

There was no way she was asking Mr. Hicks anything, the state he was in. He'd been angry before but never at her. He was more agitated this morning than she'd ever seen him. That phone call from the congressman had set something off that put him in a frenzy. She'd been hard at work since he ran out of the office and shouted at her.

She was used to him blowing up. She'd seen him lose his temper with his two security guys. She'd even seen him roar at clients, and it seemed to her, eavesdropping through the wall that separated the reception area from his office, that many of his phone conversations were held at high volume as well. Especially if he was talking to his teenage daughter. But he got over these bursts of anger pretty quickly, and she had soon learned to ignore them.

Other than that, he was a pretty decent boss. She was well-paid, and he didn't mind when she had to take time off for stuff like dentist appointments or when she had to run her mother to the doctor. Mostly, she liked how he never came on to her. Never once had he grabbed her ass or said anything that made her uncomfortable. At her last job at a big box store, she'd spent much of her time avoiding her immediate supervisor for that reason.

She had seen Seth giving her the eye a time or two when he thought she wasn't looking, but he spoke to her in a sweet way, nothing suggestive. Just playing around. She didn't mind that. In fact, she really wouldn't mind if he did try to grab her ass.

Seth emerged from the office to start folding more cartons together while she fed red-tabbed files into the pair of shredders that sat against the wall behind her desk. The shredders were big industrial models. They were loud as they chewed through the fat files, devouring paper and staples. Even over the crunch and grind of the steel teeth and through the office door, she could hear Mr. Hicks shouting at someone else. It was either Dewey or someone else with a "fat ass" that he was urging to get to the office ASAP.

With a carton in her arms, she came around the desk to meet Seth at the door.

"Are we moving or closing down?" she asked.

"I'd say this is your last day of work, honey." He took the carton from her and walked it to the open trunk of the Mercedes, which was already full. She stood in the open doorway, hugging herself against the cold, watching him set the carton on the roof of the car. He opened a rear door to place the carton inside.

"Hold the door for me." Mr. Hicks approached from behind her, a carton in his arms. It was piled high with hard drives, cell phones, a framed picture of Kathie-Beth at six dressed as a princess, and an autographed baseball in a Lucite box that the boss treasured.

"Mr. Hicks?"

He ignored her, shouldering past to hand the carton to Seth, who stuffed it in the back seat. Mr. Hicks stepped back to her, digging inside a coat pocket. He came up with a white business envelope he pressed into her hands.

"Don't report this on your taxes," he said with a brittle smile before trotting to the Mercedes. Seth was already behind the wheel. Mr. Hicks opened the passenger side door.

"Mr. Hicks!" she called after him. "I don't have the keys to lock up!"

"Fuck it!" he said and disappeared inside the car, slamming the door behind him. Spraying rock salt, the Mercedes took off in a blue cloud of exhaust.

Lynette returned to the warm lobby. The room was in chaos, with papers and streams of confetti from the shredder littering the floor. She picked up an unused carton and began placing her personal effects in it. Before setting the envelope inside, she peeled up the flap to take a peek at the contents.

It was stuffed with hundreds. What looked like hundreds of them.

She teared up a little as she riffled the bills. She'd miss this job.

———

"SON OF A BITCH," Justin Hicks seethed. He pulled a cell phone from his ear and tossed it on the dash.

"Something I can do, boss?" Seth piloted the Mercedes through the maze of the professional park.

"Fucking Dewey's not answering." Hicks started dialing a different phone, expecting better results. "The fat fuck is late, and I need to tell him where to meet us."

"Where's that we're meeting him?"

"The Target parking lot on University. But we're not meeting him if he's not answering." Hicks listened, blinking his eyes in rhythm to the ringing coming from the speaker.

"You mind telling me the plan from there?"

"That's need to know."

"Your call, boss." Seth shrugged. He piloted them around a turn lined with the ass-end of parked cars on either side. A truck was coming his way off the professional park exit. Seth pulled closer to the right to allow it passage on the narrow lane.

On the sixteenth ring, someone picked up the phone.

"Dewey! You fat fuck! Where have you—" Hicks began.

"Sir, this is Deputy Ben Ramos, Madison County Sheriff's department."

The truck, a jacked-up Chevy with a railroad-tie front bumper, was barreling toward them. Seth jerked the wheel to the right. His right front quarter panel scraped the rear bumper of a Volvo.

"What the fuck!" Hicks exclaimed.

"Sir?" the officer on the phone asked.

"Oh, shit," Seth said.

The Chevy juked to hit the Mercedes dead center in an impact that lifted the back end of the sedan off the asphalt. Windows shattered, and glass cubes showered in all directions in silver sprays. The truck plowed the Merc backward to carom off a row of parked cars with a shriek of metal on metal.

The truck halted while the sedan, engine dead now, front end crushed, rolled to a stop against a curb. It left a steaming trail of engine fluids in its wake. Bits of glass in the slush. Strips of chrome lay atop the decorative hedges like decorations. The Avalanche that had caused the destruction appeared untouched except for a dent in the timber of its improvised bumper.

Seth Tyler was dazed and gagging. The air was thick with the fine dust of talc and sodium azide from the side and front airbags explosions. The seat had been driven forward off its tracks by the force of the crash, pinning him against the wheel. He tilted his head back to see the collapsing bag. His face was slick with blood from his nose, and his mouth was filled with copper. The car listed to the right, and he heard the passenger door open.

He turned his head in time to look at the boss. Mr. Hicks, covered in a patina of fine powder, looked like a ghost in a play. A gloved hand grabbed Hicks by the collar and pulled him out of the car. He blinked through the haze to wipe away the powdery dust from inside the windshield. A big white dude in a camouflage coat was hauling Mr. Hicks to the Chevy truck. The boss was swinging his arms and trying to pull out of the bigger man's grip, but the guy kept on going, holding the boss up high enough so only the toes of his cowboy boots scraped the ground. It reminded Seth of a mom hauling her crying kid out of a toy store.

Seth struggled with the seat belt latch pressed tight around his gut. His head hurt, and his neck felt like it was on fire. He freed himself from the belt, only to find his door wedged tight from the stress of the accident.

"Accident, my ass," he said to himself as the Chevy backed away and turned for the exit.

28

Vince Holland had meant to park somewhere with an oblique view of the house. That lasted until he saw a county car with lights twirling parked at the end of the Hicks drive.

He pulled onto the brick apron, and a deputy approached from the county car to wave him away. Vince flashed his badge and ID.

"What's going on?" Vince stepped out of his car.

"Homicide," the deputy said. "Daughter came home and found a body in the driveway."

"The homeowner?"

"Don't know." The deputy shrugged. "Ambulance just got here."

Vince thanked him and pulled up the drive. Once around a sweeping curve through the trees, he could see the front of the mini-mansion, as well as two more county cars, an ambulance, and fire rescue. All had lights spinning, and the crosstalk of their radios echoed off the surrounding trees. He pulled up near where an Escalade had brodied off the drive.

"We're waiting on the sheriff and the county MEs," a

young deputy told Vince. His plastic ID badge said he was B. Ramos.

"It's not the homeowner," Vince said. The body on the drive was a big boy, well over six feet—when he still had a head.

"We're trying to contact them now."

"Any witnesses?"

"The daughter saw a white guy driving the father's SUV out onto Hobbs Island. Could be car theft. We got a BOLO on the car."

"You get a lot of that in this neighborhood? Car-jackings gone wrong?"

"Naw," the deputy said, shaking his head. "But I seen a lot of shit I never saw before I took this job."

"I want to talk to the daughter. She inside?" Vince nodded at the house.

"Be my guest." Deputy Ramos smirked and walked to the door with the marshal.

Kathie-Beth Hicks was less than useless as a witness, as most eyewitnesses were.

He found her in the kitchen, where one of the EMTs was making himself useful, trying to get her to calm down. She could barely interrupt her crying jag long enough to answer Vince's questions. The best he could get from her was that the deceased had worked for her father. Her description of the guy driving her dad's SUV was vague at best.

Vince returned to his car to get on the horn to Bo Charles, who was en route to Hicks' office to keep an eye on the lawyer's comings and goings. He moved past the poorly parked Escalade and noticed the LoJack decal in a lower corner of the driver's side window. He called Bo Charles as he trotted back to Deputy Ramos.

A voice on his phone. "Go for Charles."

"Hold on, bro," Vince said, then told Ramos, "The stolen car will have LoJack. Get up on that, all right?"

The deputy nodded and leaned into the open window of his unit to get on the horn.

"We got a homicide here at the Hicks residence," Vince said to Bo Charles.

"And we got a clusterfuck at the lawyer's office. A hit and run that might be an abduction." Bo Charles sounded out of breath.

"The fuck?"

"Some guy in a pickup totaled Hicks' Mercedes, then took off with Hicks."

"Was he alone?"

"The guy?"

"No! Hicks!"

"A guy works for him, a brother, he was driving. He's pretty banged up. They got an ambo coming."

Vince turned back to the house. Deputy Ramos was calling to the other deputies. They all ran to their units to pull shotguns from the racks, then hauled ass around the side of the house, heading north like the start of a marathon.

"Stay on it!" Vince said and stuffed the phone in his coat pocket. He ran after the deputies.

———

BO CHARLES TRIED to talk to the man still seated behind the wheel of the ruined Mercedes. The guy was in and out of it, mostly concerned with getting his ass out of the car. He'd taken a serious hit to the head and had a nasty gash across the bridge of his nose. The cartilage had separated. He was probably concussed. Proof positive of that was him mistaking Bo Charles for someone he knew. The marshal leaned into that.

"Motherfucker took the boss right out the car, Luther," the man behind the wheel said, his words running together.

"What the motherfucker look like?"

"Big fucker. White man. Drivin' wunna them redneck trucks."

"What color, cousin?"

"I told you! A white man!" the driver said, spraying blood from between his teeth.

That was all he could get from the man. The EMTs enforced their authority to get the driver out from behind the wheel by using a pry bar to get the jammed door off. When they pulled him out of the car and onto a backboard, an automatic fell to the ground from somewhere inside the man's clothing.

"Leave that right there," Bo Charles warned, showing his ID. "Where you taking this man?"

They told him they were taking the driver to Huntsville Memorial. After strapping his head into a cervical collar, they lifted the driver onto the gurney with some effort. He was a big one. Bo Charles spoke to the deputies who'd arrived on the scene while the driver was loaded into the ambulance and advised them to start treating this as a crime scene.

Bo spoke to some of the folks who'd come out of the buildings to take a gander at the action. They'd seen everything and nothing. The truck was either burgundy, black, or chocolate. No one really saw much of the driver, but all remarked on how the smaller man had fought like a fish on a hook for all the good it did him. Two of the more reliable lookie-loos, a cute little dental hygienist and an older woman who was late for a podiatry appointment, had had a clear view of the rear of the truck. The hygienist had been taking a smoke break between buildings and the old lady had been in her car, having pulled in behind the truck. They agreed that the bigger man had dropped the covered tailgate of the truck, shoved the smaller man inside, and locked him in. They didn't remember the plate number.

With nothing to do but wait for county detectives, Bo Charles slipped on vinyl gloves and returned to the wrecked Merc. He took a picture of the dropped weapon with his phone: a Sig in a tooled leather clip-on. Nicer than his service piece.

The windows of the car were all gone except for a fringe of glass, allowing him to reach inside the back seat. There were some open cardboard cartons there. They'd spilled their contents all over the seats and floor. He poked through the mess, careful not to cut his fingers on any of the glass beads that covered everything.

A baseball signed by Carl Yastrzemski. A picture of a little girl in braces wearing a white dress and tiara in a cracked frame. A whole lot of cell phones and some aluminum and black plastic boxes with ports down one edge. In the popped trunk was another carton packed with paper files, all marked with yellow tabs.

Two Madison County CID men arrived twenty minutes later to find waiting for them the happiest US marshal they'd ever seen in their lives.

29

Wesley Ruskin woke up before dawn, soaked in sweat despite the chill. He sat up in darkness and quiet and unnatural blackness, with no sky above. A dead, lifeless quiet. He stayed where he was, frozen, eyes searching until he saw a faint gray light describing the frames of the windows that ran across the front of the double-wide. He recalled then where he was and why there were no stars above or forest noises.

Rising from the cot in the center of the main room, he took off his sopping t-shirt and wiped himself clean with a cloth at the bathroom sink. After a breakfast of fried eggs and sausage, he dressed for the pre-dawn cold to spend the morning exploring the grounds and outbuildings that surrounded the former Klan hideout.

A small herd of deer lifted their antlered heads at the sight of him, then exploded into motion. Within seconds, they were gone into the greater blackness of the trees that lined the sides of the broad holler floor.

Milkweed and coggins grass grew thick everywhere, brown and drooping in the winter chill. Out back of the main building, he found a steel swing set and a slide crusted with orange rust in the knee-high growth of weeds. Back in the day, the crackers must have brought kids up in here to get them started early with their hateful bullshit.

As he got closer to the tree line, he came upon some old cars left that had been left to rot. A Dodge pickup nearly seventy years old, crusted with rust. A Camaro like one an uncle of his had owned was up on concrete blocks, black with mold. An ancient International Harvester tractor and some kind of tiller or mower setup they probably used to keep the grass down.

Place had probably looked like a damned picnic park once upon a time. That was back in the days when the Klan was still a power in the South. His older relatives told him about those days. It all sounded to him like more than a different time; it sounded like a different *world*. He'd often wondered if they weren't exaggerating. Growing up, he had seen little of the kind of racism they claimed had been as much a part of their lives as the weather. Sure, he'd been called a nigger and a coon a few times by kids in school. It was name-calling and nothing more than that, same as if he'd been fat or had pimples or a speech impediment. Kids were cruel. Bullies used any distinguishing feature to pick on their victims. Could be a kid wearing glasses or the wrong brand of sneakers. Or his skin color.

Truth was, the only times he could remember being called a nigger, it was migrant kids doing it. He'd call them beaners and greasers in turn. Kids ranking on each other. One time it had gotten serious; some Mexican kids started in on him when he rode his bike to the 7-Eleven near his grandma's house. They knocked him down in the parking lot and shoved him off his bike onto the asphalt. Cherry Slurpee went all over, staining a brand-new white tee and soaking his jeans. He'd kept a grip on his bike while the kids, laughing and calling him dirty names, tried to pull it from his grasp.

It was Will Parrish who'd stepped in to help him. Will was a white boy from his school that he only knew from gym class. Big boy who went on to play college ball before dying in a car accident before he was twenty. He and Wesley were hardly friends, yet Will was there beside him out of nowhere. He'd shoved the migrant kids away from the bike, and Wesley had wrenched the bike out of their grip. One of the Mexicans had tumbled in back of a Ford pickup pulling out of a space in front of the store. The guy had slammed on his brakes and gotten out of the cab to yell at them.

The kids had scattered then. Wesley had pedaled away in one direction, and Will had run in another. He saw Will a few times around the school after that. Never did thank him for that day.

The sky was lightening from gray to salmon as he picked his way among the derelict vehicles turning to piles of rust in the trees. He saw a rectangular shape out of place in the gloom. From twenty feet or more into the trees, he could see it was the plane of a corrugated metal roof. A structure of cinder blocks the size of a lawn-mower shed was built into the slope of the holler. It was sheltered by the lowest boughs of old pines.

This shed was the most substantial structure he'd seen on the property. The portion of the block wall exposed above the earthen bank was painted in roofing tar. The door was metal in a steel frame, secured with a padlock powdered white with corrosion. Someone didn't want any prying eyes taking a peek inside.

Wesley searched the ground until he found a rock the size of his fist. Three hard slams and the hasp parted from the doorframe with a screech of metal. Time and oxidation had fixed the door in place as if it had been welded shut. He went back to the main building and came back with an axe handle and a pry bar. He wedged the tooth of the bar into the gap between the door and frame, loosening a rain of red dust. Running the axe handle through the pull handle gave him some leverage. He worked up a fresh sweat pushing the bar back and forth until the door popped at a top corner. He worked the pry down from there until the door came away from the frame. The top hinge gave under the weight, the set screws breaking to leave the door sagging in front of the dark opening.

Before his eyes could adjust to the darkness within, he could smell the contents of the shed. It was a pungent mix of odors from maybe decades of being trapped inside. These were smells he knew well from his time in the service.

"Shit the bed," Wesley said under his breath.

The sweet scent of rotten bananas meant dynamite.

A strong oily stink with a tinge of fecal matter. That was C-4 or one of its cousins. Semtex or the like.

He poked his head through the doorway.

The shed had a concrete floor. Wood shelves with steel uprights lined two of the walls. Two wooden crates sat on the lowest shelf, with military surplus metal ammo containers on the other shelves. He touched his fingertips to the shelf under the crates. The surface was dusty with rust but not crusted. The shed had been built to remain dry. Set as it was into the hillside, it would remain cool as well. According to the markings on the crates, the contents were #3 dynamite. They were from the Redstone Arsenal and had been the property of the Army Corps of Engineers at one time. There were plastic snap cases on the shelves that, he guessed, probably held detonators or det cord or both.

Taking great care not to create any sparks, he

replaced the door in the frame as best he could before backing down the hill back to the main building.

———

HE WAS CARRYING a box to the trash pit when he heard a vehicle approaching through the trees. A knotted muscle between his shoulders relaxed when he recognized Levon Cade's Avalanche rolling up the drive.

He dumped the box onto the growing heap of crap he'd cleared from inside his new home. There were stacks of yellowed flyers bound in twine and back issues of the tabloid papers *White Lightning* and *Shotgun News*, along with other debris left behind by men long gone. Clothing, flags, broken furniture, a portable TV with blown tubes, and a stack of Budweiser cases full of empties. He'd also found a near-complete collection of *Playboys* from 1962 to 1971 on a shelf inside the closet he was using as a bedroom. Those he kept.

Levon backed the truck to the door of the double-wide and cut the engine. Wesley walked up to meet him.

"I got chili on. Should be done in another hour or so if you're stayin' awhile," Wesley said.

"I'll be here awhile. How you getting along?" Levon looked tired, like he'd been on the run around the clock.

"Almost done getting this place livable. Already better than a groundsheet in the woods, though. Cold rain up here last night. I was glad to be out of it. Hold on."

Wesley heard a muffled voice from somewhere inside the truck and a drumming sound from the covered truck bed. Someone was back there, kicking away at the tonneau cover.

"You bring company?"

Levon nodded.

"Hope he likes chili."

THE INTERIOR of the double-wide was warm, thanks to a wood stove Wesley had put back into operation. Adding to the warmth was the stockpot bubbling on the stovetop and the pan of cornbread turning brown in the oven. The simmering chili filled the air with spice.

The place was cleaner now. With most of the boxes and broken furniture removed, the smell of must was gone, replaced by the scent of the pine cleaner Wesley had used to scrub down every surface of the kitchen. The Klan flag, posters, and framed photos had been removed from the paneled walls. The Stars and Bars remained on the wall next to a newly hung American flag.

"You kept the rebel flag," Levon said.

"That don't bother me so much." Wesley shrugged. "Never missed *Dukes of Hazzard* when I was a kid."

Wesley looked at the contents of the two equipment bags spread out on the tabletop. Levon was sorting through it, making neat stacks of bundled cash, paper files, CDs, and ledgers.

"This all from selling kids to perverts?" Wesley picked up a thick stack of bills bound with rubber bands.

"Not directly," Levon said. "He's a facilitator. A connection into the foster care system. Just another guy with his hand out."

"Some hand." The stack Wesley held was all twenties. A thousand dollars, maybe. There were other stacks of hundreds and fifties. Wesley looked at the man they'd taken out of the back of the Avalanche. He sat on a folding chair against a wall, ankles and wrists zip-tied, with one loop run to the chair frame to keep him in place. The guy was giving them a defiant look that was starting to fray around the edges and mouthing away through a double layer of duct tape slapped over his mouth.

"What we doin' here, Levon?"

"I want to hold him a few days while I work some things out. You can babysit him for me?"

"What you call babysitting, the law calls kidnapping. You ain't law."

"No. I'm not law." Levon looked up from the work of sorting.

"So, what we doin' here?"

"I never put it into words before."

"Give it a try."

"You have something to drink here, Wesley?"

"You know I do." Wesley got them each a Heinie from the fridge.

Levon took a long pull. He looked at the man seated against the wall, then at Wesley across the table piled with cash.

"I got in trouble when I came back. I took on a job I shouldn't have to help out a friend. Been in trouble ever since, all of my own making. Maybe it's a burden I have to carry."

"That's telling me jack shit." Wesley tapped the bottom of his bottle against a pile of bills, spilling some bundles off the top. "You show up here with all this money and some guy tied up and tell me he's a child molester. I need more than that to go off of."

Levon shared with him the story of his cousin Teddy Lee and the disappearance of Teddy's son. He told how this had led him to look for the boy and to a house where a man local to his county kept other boys as prisoners for the kind of men who like children. At the house, he'd uncovered videotapes of those men going back years. Some of them were highly placed in politics and business across the southeast.

"You coulda' handed all that over to the police. Or the FBI," Wesley said.

"You see this guy?" Levon nodded at their guest. "He's been operating for years. Almost as long as Coach Sherwood. And just like the coach, he's had people covering for him. I give all those tapes to the sheriff or the feds, and I might as well burn them for all the good it'll do."

"This is vigilante stuff. In the eyes of the law, you're just as much a criminal as this one."

They went outside and sat under the picnic portico, away from the mewling and the stifled roars of the attorney.

"You're right. I know that, only I also know there's two kinds of law. There's the kind you and me either abide by or break and pay whatever price for the choices we make. Then there's the law for people like this guy. And from all I've seen, that's no law at all."

Wesley drained his beer and rose to toss the empty into a carton he was using for trash. He popped the top off another beer and turned back to Levon.

"And the money? No matter what this fool's done, you're still stealin'."

"I'll drop that somewhere. Salvation Army or a church."

"You think that makes it right? That squares things?"

"If you'd seen the things I saw. If you saw the house where I got the tapes I found."

"This what you brought me outta the holler for? To be your accomplice?"

"Nothing like that. I'd have brought him here anyway. I told you to make this place your home, and I meant that and nothing else. It's up to you. I can take him away and go find another place to stash him. Up to you."

"Let's hear what *he* has to say." Wesley went inside and tore the tape off the captive man's mouth.

Justin Hicks took a gulp from the beer bottle offered him and went into his pitch without being questioned. He started by offering to allow the men to keep the cash they'd taken if they set him free, but he'd need all the files back or no deal. When neither man leapt at the offer, he moved from deal-making to threats that were at first vague, then more specific. He warned them that by abducting him, they had made themselves some very powerful enemies. Hicks swore he knew people in the governors' offices in four states. He knew millionaires, people that were local celebrities, who could make anyone's life hell. If they tried to make use of any of the information they'd stolen, both of them would pay. Their families, too. They'd all be lucky if they were killed quickly. If they let him go today, right now, all would be forgiven, and the cash would be theirs.

Wesley tore a fresh length of duct tape off the roll. Hicks sputtered while Wesley wound the tape around his head to seal his mouth once more. He continued squealing as Wesley walked to the kitchen.

"Hope you like your chili hot. And I put okra in it."

"Corn too?"

"I put kernels in the cornbread batter."

"Hillbilly chili," Levon said. "Sounds good to me."

30

Laura Strand, caffeinated to the eyeballs, set the cruise control ten miles above the speed limit and headed north on 65 for Huntsville.

She directed Vince Holland and Tony Marcoon over the rental's OnStar.

The hit and run in the professional park and the homicide at the Hicks house had made waiting for the warrant irrelevant. Both those places were active crime scenes, so all the evidence contained within the house and the Mercedes was up for grabs. The evidence chain was locked down as property of the US marshals and Laura assumed lead over all of it.

Someone with a hard-on for Justin Hicks had spent a busy morning, from the murder of the bodyguard at the house and the presumed theft of a family car to the obvious abduction and vehicular assault in the professional park. Both places had yielded oodles of physical evidence to support a case for criminal conspiracy under RICO.

The hard drives and phones found in the back of the Merc were already on the way to Quantico, bagged and tagged and in the custody of Bo Charles. He was heading to the airport for a Delta flight to BWI. The devices would be encrypted, cataloged, and transcribed there. Laura knew in her bones they would tell quite the story and lead to multiple arrests if the participants were not already boogying after getting word about Hicks' home invasion and the fender bender.

"Someone sure took a big greasy shit on our case." Tony Marcoon's whiskey voice came through the speakers on the dash to sum things up.

"Starting with the judge. Let's hope we can establish a contact between him and Hicks on one of those phones." Laura gunned above her cruise limit to pass a long semi-trailer throwing up a wash of filthy snowmelt from all eighteen wheels.

"Man, I'd love to get that asshole's balls in a vice," Marcoon said, followed by a sotto voce apology to someone there with him.

"Tony, where are you?"

"In an elevator at the hospital. Tyler's coming out of the OR."

"This is the driver of the Merc?"

"Seth Tyler. Long list of priors up north. He broke a leg and a couple of ribs. Bad break. Two pins and a plate."

"He'll be woozy."

"Like truth serum." She heard the ding of a bell and the rattle of elevator doors opening in the background.

"His lawyers will use that to throw out anything he says," Laura said.

"For all the good it'll do them. We have him dead bang for whatever's on those hard drives they were so anxious to pull. So, I can wait to talk to him or pump him for anything helpful now. Up to you, boss."

"Pump him. I'm two hours out. If you get anything useful, send the audio file to my phone."

"Will do."

"I have another call." Laura cut him off to take the call from Vince Holland.

"What do you have for me, Vince?"

"Me and Spaz are at the house. Bo Charles handed the hit and run off to Rizzo and Mountain. County is on the scene doing prints, and state CID is on the way. Everyone's cooperating and playing nice for now. Not sure how long that'll hold up once the staties show up."

"Have Tony handle them, homicide cop to homicide cop. What's your first take at the house?"

"Positive ID on the victim. What I can see and what we get out of the daughter, it looks like the vic, one..." Vince looked at his notes, "Leonard DeWalt Bascomb, was ambushed outside. One of the family cars, a '19 Cadillac Escalade, was stolen off the driveway. The daughter says she saw it driven by a man she doesn't know shortly before getting home to find Bascomb dead. We found the Escalade at an adjoining property."

"That means a second car. This was a hit."

"Looks pretty professional to me, boss," Vince said. "From the looks of the house, our boy Hicks was planning on a run. Two safes in the house were mostly cleaned out and left open like no one was coming back."

"Where's the stuff?"

"I think we can safely assume it was in the Escalade. My guess, given what we know of the timeline here? Someone waited for Bascomb to finish loading up before popping him."

"That's cold. Nothing on the second vehicle?"

"County cops are canvassing the other houses, but this is a pretty rural setback. The houses are on large lots with lots of trees. Chances of anyone eye-deeing the getaway car pretty much suck."

"We'll check CC and hope for the best. That all you have?"

"That's all, boss."

"Stay on it, Vince."

"Till the hunt's over, boss."

She cut him off to call Marshal Jake Tetley, AKA Mountain. He reported much the same. He and Andy Rizzo had taken lead, but the deputies were on the scene to go over the car. Mountain and Rizzo were doing their own canvass for witnesses, starting with the offices of Heart and Home. Lynette Anne Holmes was not happy to see them.

"We took an envelope stuffed fulla cash off her," Mountain said through the speakers with a deep basso voice that matched his massive stature. "She pitched a fit. That was her severance pay is what she told us. Rizzo dealt with her while I bagged it. He told her we were within our rights to cuff her and take her in. She got quiet after that."

"Will she cooperate?"

"Too early to say. The deputies are holding her for us as a material witness. Me or Rizzo will talk to her when we leave here. Probably Rizzo. I think he wants to propose."

"Anything on the hit-and-run vehicle?"

"Big old redneck war wagon. Pickup with a covered bed. Some said it was a Chevy. One guy said it was a Toyota. They're all over the map on color, but it narrows down to dark red."

"Plates?"

"You know the story. 'It all happened so fast!'"

"Driver?"

"Big guy. White. Lean build. Dressed like a construction worker. Pretty generic."

"Did Hicks struggle or go along with him easy?"

"Fought like a cat. A dental hygienist is our best witness so far. She says the big guy clocked Hicks a good one. He calmed down after that. Then the driver zip-tied his wrists and ankles and tossed him into the back of the truck."

"The back seat?"

"The bed. Like a bag of trash is how she put it."

31

"I need to piss," Justin Hicks announced.

The men seated at the table turned his way.

"Unless you want to mop it up."

The black guy rose from the table and used a clasp knife to cut the plastic strip that secured Justin's wrists to the standpipe, then the strip that hobbled his ankles. His legs were asleep from being motionless for so long. The black man helped him to his feet and, with a strong grip on his arm, guided him toward the door.

"I said I need the bathroom."

"Bathroom's outside."

The black guy shouldered the door open to pull him out into the cold air. Justin looked back to see the white guy clearing the table of bowls, silverware, and beer empties. All his cash sat neatly stacked on one end of the table where they'd counted it out. Just shy of seven hundred thousand. The black guy marched him around the double-wide to a narrow shack that sat on a raised platform a good thirty paces out back.

"An outhouse?" Justin said.

"Like a porta-potty that don't go nowhere. You need me to tell you how to work it?"

"No. I've seen them. In movies."

Inside the gloom of the outhouse, Justin struggled to undo his pants with his wrists bound together. He shucked his khakis and underwear down and took a seat on the cold hard bench. His eyes adjusted to the light coming down through the rippled translucent roof. All he found inside was a wrinkled back issue of *Penthouse* and a damp roll of two-ply. At least it was too cold for the shack to smell. Much.

His options looked grim. Even if he got away from this pair, he had no idea where he was. From the hour-long drive and what he'd seen when the white guy took him out of the bed of the truck, he was deep in the country. Nothing but trees and empty sky. He took another look around the confines of the shitter for anything that might be of use as a weapon, then scoffed at that idea. Both of his captors were way bigger than him.

Though, he thought as sweet relief came to his bladder, he did have a weapon after all.

"That's a lot of money," he said while the black guy walked behind him to the house.

No answer.

"It's all yours if you help me get away, brother."

"My brother's black."

"Come on. You know what I mean. You believe what that guy told you? I'm some kind of gangster?"

"He never called you no gangster. He said you rape kids."

"I've never done that. I'm not like that." Justin lowered his voice as they walked along a wall of the double-wide toward the front. "I'm an adoption lawyer."

"You're a lawyer for people who rape kids."

"It's not like that." They were nearing the front door,

and the customer wasn't buying. "Look, you're in a lot of trouble here, you know that? You're in deep shit, and you're just too dumb to see it."

"*I'm* in trouble?" The black guy pulled the door open and took a handful of Justin's shirt to haul him inside.

The white guy sat on the opposite side of the table. A bowl of red slop and a plate with a cake of yellow bread were next to him.

"Eat something while we talk," the white guy said.

The black guy dropped Justin in a folding chair and pushed him closer to the table.

"Beer, Coke, or water?" the black guy asked.

"What kind of water?" Justin asked.

The black guy made a sound with his lips and walked to the kitchen to return with a can of Coke. The white guy picked up a phone and held the screen out at Justin. He thought at first the guy was going to snap his picture, like for a ransom demand. Instead, the white guy handed Justin the phone. On the screen, a video was playing. In the video, a man with his back to the camera was removing his shirt while speaking to someone off-screen. The responses were in the voice of a child. When the man moved out of the foreground, the room came into view. A boy, maybe ten or eleven, in a Star Wars t-shirt and tighty whities sat on a sofa in a room with faded flocked wallpaper in the background.

Justin's stomach turned. He looked away.

"Look at it. You know the man in this video?" the white guy asked.

"You got the money. There's more I can get you. I can tell you where there's lots more."

"Do you know the name of the man in this video?"

Justin held the phone in his bound hands and narrowed his eyes as though studying the image. His thoughts raced to all the doorways in his mind to search for ways out of this. One by one, he pulled the doors open. Nothing here. Not this one. Not this one, either. All the while, the moving images on the phone blurred before him. The rhythmic grunts and pained squeals from the tinny phone speaker filled his ears. He damned sure did know the man on the phone. The boy too, for that matter.

"I've never seen either of them before in my life," he said, voice level and eyes fixed on the white guy's cold gaze.

The white guy plucked the phone from his fingers to tap and swipe at the screen. The black guy sat sipping at a Coke, regarding Justin with only mild interest.

"How about this man? You know him?" The white guy held out the phone in a rough hand for him to see the screen. A different room. A different child, this one younger. An adult male, speaking endearments and soft words of encouragement, moved into the frame and turned until his face was visible.

Justin's vision swam. He took his eyes off the screen to look down at a puddle of grease shimmering above the lumpy mess in the bowl. Deep in his guts, he felt the clench of a fist.

He broke out in a sweat. "I think I need the bathroom again."

"You know this man?" the white guy asked, tilting the phone to bring it into his line of vision.

Justin turned his face away. "Seriously, I think I might be sick."

"How about you, Wesley? You know this man?" The white guy tossed the phone to the black guy, who cast eyes on the moving image on the screen.

"Damn sure do," the black guy said, his eyes going hard.

"I really need to go back to the outhouse." The fist in Justin's belly twisted, its grip tightening.

"That's *you*. That's you on that phone, Mr. I'm-a-lawyer-who-don't-rape-kids," the black guy said, each word drawing the knot in Justin's guts that much tighter.

"Are you beginning to appreciate the seriousness of your situation yet?" the white guy asked.

The fist released its hold, and Justin felt a sudden rush.

"God damn," the black guy said, clapping a hand over his nose and mouth.

"I told you I needed the bathroom," Justin said, his eyes filling with hot tears.

32

"You mind me saying that you look like hell?" Tony Marcoon said.

Laura Strand dropped her attaché case in a chair to pace the floor of the office the sheriff was letting the marshals use. "You mentioned something about a politician?"

"Turns out it's a congressman. Seriously, you look beat, boss."

"Didn't sleep much last night. Now I'm not sure I can. A congressman?"

"House of Representatives, tenth district," Tony read from his notebook. "This Seth Tyler mentioned it. The receptionist told him, or he overheard it. The guy was drugged up post-surgery. In and out. I checked with the receptionist, and she gave me the name. Phillip Burns. He's been in office since before color TV."

"And what's his connection?" Laura pulled open drawers. "Any aspirins in here?" A caffeine headache compounded by three hours of driving in winter glare had settled behind her eyes.

"He called to speak to Hicks right before Hicks

started packing for Mexico. Here." Tony tossed her a bottle of Advil. "He called on a landline, so we'll have a record of it. Hicks probably called back on a burner, but we might have bagged that out of the Merc. Are Post-it notes admissible evidence? The receptionist wrote down the rep's name and the time of the first call."

"We'll set a precedent." Laura took four Advil and popped them one at a time, swallowing them dry.

"I could never do that," Tony remarked as she downed the last one.

"Bitter," she said and made a "come on" gesture with her hand. Tony flipped to a new page.

"We got near *nada* on traffic cams. Huntsville is not exactly wired up for surveillance. We have one shot of a truck that might be the suspect in the background of a red-light monitor. The truck is moving north on a surface road that could have taken him anywhere."

"The red-light cam catch a license plate?"

"No luck there. Bad angle. He was moving lateral across the shot."

"Did you ask about anyone who might have it in for Hicks?"

"The bodyguard just smiled at that one. According to the receptionist, everyone loved him. Vince is bringing the daughter in, but my guess is she'll offer us no revelations."

"Theories?" Laura plopped into a chair to lean her elbows on the desk and massage her temples.

"Competitor? Someone he cheated? The guy's a lawyer. They collect enemies like my brother-in-law collects golf tees."

"What are the chances this ties into that string of other killings? This guy's in the middle of a trafficking operation. Maybe it ties to our concerned citizen. Could be it all started up long before we took this on."

"So, maybe we kill time on background? If we wait long enough, this guy in the truck could clean house for us."

"I don't like playing catch-up, Tony. This guy's been ahead of us all the way."

"We keep on, then. This guy has to have fucked up somewhere. Or we'll cross his path. Whichever comes first."

"I have this tiny little bell ringing in my head," Laura said, her hands over her aching eyes. "Either I need twelve hours sleep, or I'm trying to tell myself something."

"Go to the hotel, then," Tony said. "Get some sleep. We'll have more to work on later tonight."

"What would I do without you?" She pushed to her feet.

As she left the room, he called, "And no coffee!"

———

HE HATED HOSPITALS. Hated the smell of them.

When Tony Marcoon was five and in the Children's Hospital to get his tonsils out, the place had smelled like rubbing alcohol. Fifteen years back, when his mom was in her last days at Fox Chase, the place had smelled like carbolic.

Seth Tyler's room smelled like industrial disinfectant losing its fight to cover the scent of aged piss. Tony didn't want to be here, but with Laura crashed out and the muscle beach marshals pursuing further leads, he was the only one of the team on tap.

Tyler was coming out of his propofol haze and sitting up as comfortably as he could with his leg in a heavy cast and slung on a traction rig. His left arm was cuffed to the bedrail, and just in case, a county deputy, a freckled-faced kid who didn't look old enough to drink, was parked in a chair against the window.

"You need me to leave the room?" the deputy asked, starting to rise.

"You can stay." Tony pulled aside the rolling cart on which sat an untouched dinner tray of mystery meat with mac and cheese. "Not hungry, Tyler?"

"Don't eat that hospital shit." Tyler looked him up and down. "Who're you?"

"It's not good, but you'd better get used to eating shit. US marshal." Tony flashed his badge and ID. He picked up the remote and killed the volume on the wall-mounted TV. Two guys and a girl talking about upcoming bowl games. He put his phone, set to record, atop the tray cover.

"The time is 6:42 PM, December 30. Anthony Marcoon to question Seth Tyler with—" Tony turned to the deputy. "What's your name?"

"Gary Meyers, badge number 289," the deputy said, half rising from his chair before Tony waved him back.

"With Madison County Deputy Sheriff Gary Meyers, badge number 289 in attendance."

"Why I got to be cuffed?" Tyler pulled the cuff chain taut with a tug. "Motherfucker hit *me* and took the boss away."

"Your boss know this guy?"

"How'm I supposed to know? I don't know everyone he knows."

"You just drive the car. And that piece we took off you is for shooting snakes, am I right?"

"I got a permit for that."

"I gotta wonder how you managed that with your record. Your boss has some pull, right? Like the congressman you told me about."

Tyler's eyes narrowed.

"Told you what? I never told you shit. I ain't never seen you before."

"This morning. After they brought you out of the OR."

"Bullshit."

"Don't worry, none of that's on the record. Your employer, Justin Hicks, is connected. Connected how?"

"He's a lawyer. Know all kinds of people. Businessmen and all like that."

"How's he know them?"

"What's any of this got to do with me?" Tyler made to sit up, his busted leg swinging in its hammock rig. He winced.

"That's what I'm trying to find out. Your boss is under investigation for child trafficking and gets a phone call just as we're getting ready to federal warrant his ass. He's off to Rio with a carload of hard drives and cell phones, and you're the one driving the car. You know what 'accessory' means, right?"

"Accessory to *what*? I'm just the nigga behind the wheel."

"You can't *be* this stupid. You're transporting evidence in a capital offense case. Trafficking minor children. We're looking through those hard drives and phones. We find the kind of video or images on there I think we're gonna find, and you're up on charges for baby rape. You've done time. You know what it's like for baby-rapers inside. Now ramp that up to eleven for a federal lockup."

"I want a lawyer." Tyler pretended interest in a commercial for a Caribbean resort island on the muted TV.

"You *had* a lawyer until someone took him. That was some bodyguarding, Seth."

"That guy head-on'ed us! What was I supposed to do to stop that?"

"You're lucky he didn't blow half your head off like he did your partner."

"What the fuck you talkin' about?"

"Your buddy Bascomb back at the house. Same guy wrecked you and took your boss killed him. Shotgun to the chest and head. Ugly scene."

"Dewey's dead?" Tyler stared at Tony, then at the deputy, who nodded gravely.

"Someone doesn't like your lawyer boss, and they're not shy about homicide. Might have something to do with the business your boss is in. Maybe they might come back around for you, seeing as you're in the same line of work."

"I don't know anything about no *pee*-do-phile shit. I drive him and watch the house. Run errands and shit like that."

"I believe you. A federal prosecutor might believe you. A jury might believe you. But this guy doesn't do any due diligence. He's got a mad on for anyone with an eye for minors. The only reason you're alive now is he thought you died in the crash."

"Bullshit." Tyler turned away, a half-smile on his lips.

"He's telling the truth." Deputy Freckles spoke up. Until that moment, he'd been watching Tony Marcoon at work like it was a crime show on the TV.

"I got this, okay?" Tony said, his brittle smile barely hiding his annoyance.

"Yeah, some dude's hunting pedos." The deputy leaned forward in his chair, eager to contribute. "Killed a whole houseful up near the Tennessee line."

"Whole houseful of what?" Tony said.

"You know. Child molesters." He pronounced it "*mo-*

lesters." "Left the kids alive. Some of 'em gone missing years back."

33

"That's all I have," Justin Hicks said. "I just want to sleep."

"Not yet," the white guy said.

The great room of the double-wide was dim except for the light coming from a fluorescent fixture over the sink in the kitchen area. The black guy was in there, busy with something.

Justin shivered with cold and pulled the blanket draped over his shoulders closer as best he could. It was difficult with only one hand free, the other zip-tied to the frame of the folding chair he'd been sitting on for the past four hours. He wore another blanket about his waist to cover his naked ass. After his accident, the two men had removed his khakis and underwear. The white guy had sprayed him clean in a stall shower. The black guy had bagged his soiled clothes and taken them outside to a barrel fire.

"What more do you want?" His voice came out in a croak.

"There's still a few men on the videos I don't have names for." The white guy ran a finger down a list he'd made. "You told me 'Cowboy Bill' is Martin Best, your accountant. And 'Zorro' is Arnold Reeves, a real estate agent out of Atlanta."

"That's right. I might remember more if you let me sleep some."

"But this 'El Capitan.' You say you recognize him but don't know his name."

"I ran into him once or twice. Maybe three times. We don't all get to know each other. It's not like it's the Lions Club."

"He only appears once in the Sherwood tapes, but you say you saw him more than once?"

Hicks tried not to look away. A liar always looks away. He met the white guy's hard gaze.

"Maybe Dads only taped him the one time."

"Maybe you met him somewhere else."

"Look, let me sleep, all right? I can't think straight."

"You're doing fine. Where else was it you ran into El Capitan?"

"I don't remember." Hicks lowered his face into shadow to hide his lie.

"Sure, you do." The white guy kicked the leg of Hicks' chair. "You damned sure remember."

Hicks swallowed hard.

"The Hacienda. I mostly saw him there."

"What's that? What's the Hacienda?"

"It's a house in Brillings. Just outside of town off the township road."

"Which Brillings? Kentucky?"

"Georgia. Randolph County."

"Where is it? What's the address?" The white guy kicked the chair leg again.

"I don't have an address, you dumb prick! You think I keep a Christmas card list?"

"You said it's outside of town off the township road. East? West?"

"North of Brillings, I think. North of Main Street. It follows the train tracks."

"Describe the house."

"It's two-story. Red siding like a barn. Set back off the road with garages in back."

"Big house? Small?"

"I guess it's a big place. Four thousand square feet, maybe."

"And it's like Sherwood's house? They keep boys there?"

"Girls too."

"The same kids or different kids?"

"They keep the stock rotated. I only get down there maybe twice a year. Different kids every time."

"Who's 'they?'"

"The Duttons. Edward and his wife, Trish. They own the house, run the shop. Can I sleep now?"

The white guy rose from where he sat across the table from Justin to go into the kitchen. The black guy was washing the pot and bowls from their chili dinner hours before. The white guy left behind his phone and the pad of paper and pen. The top sheet was covered with a neatly written list of names, some with phone numbers.

A chill settled on him. Even the heat of the wood stove wasn't taking it away. He wondered if it was a fever, if he'd caught some kind of bug. Or it could be fear.

They owned him. There was no way around that.

Damn Sherwood to hell.

That peckerwood asshole had videotaped everyone who came to his place. Men Justin knew well. Men he'd met once. Men he only knew by reputation. Others he didn't recognize but probably knew by their avatars on the different private sites. Almost all of his friends from the Corvette Club had been captured *in flagrante delicto* on the grainy old analog videos the white guy had been showing him for the past four hours.

He knew Dan Sherwood was dead. He also understood that one or both of these men was responsible. They had obviously also helped themselves to Dads' video collection. Everyone in the network had heard the details of that night last fall before it was scrubbed clean for the media and buried under bureaucracy by the state. One of the men who'd helped bury it, Phil Barnes, was featured in a video the white guy had shown him. The fat old bastard, minus his toupee and clothes, was prominently featured with an eight-year-old in a room at Sherwood's that Justin knew well.

Someone, most likely his current hosts, had gone through that house like a double dose of cod liver oil. They'd killed Sherwood, four of his customers, and a Georgia state cop. Some kids had been taken away from the place by county cops. Justin recognized their names but wondered about the absence of the boy he knew only as Sonny. There was no one of that boy's description in either the list of the deceased or the boys who had been returned to their families.

Sonny had graduated from being one of Sherwood's boys to being a chicken hawk bringing in new flesh. Justin had not visited the house in a year or more. Perhaps the boy had left Sherwood's employ since then, one way or the other.

In addition to the boys found alive at the house, the names of some of those disinterred from the cellar were familiar to him as well.

His captors had what they wanted now. He had no choice but to accommodate them. His value was zero. There was no reason for them to keep him alive.

Though, only he knew that.

"I know other names, other places," he said.

The white guy turned from his conversation with the black guy.

"What other names? What other places?"

"I told you about the Corvette Club." Justin spoke easily, forcing a tone of superiority into his voice to hint at the wealth of knowledge he'd withheld. "Not all of the members are in those movies of yours."

The Corvette Club was a cover for men, and a very few women, who shared the same predilection. They had a web page that served as a message board where they shared information on vintage Stingrays and Grand Sports and announced meets where they showed off their cars. Any uninitiated visitor who stumbled across the site and followed the directions to one of the meets would find himself the only one in attendance. The "meets" were coded arrangements for pick-ups, hook-ups, and exchanges. In reality, korvetteklubv8350.net was a virtual slave market.

"You said you wanted to sleep," the white guy said.

"I do. I'm beat. I only want you to know I have more info for you."

The white guy turned to the black guy to confer, then turned back to Justin.

"We were getting ourselves a beer. You need a beer?"

"Sure. Sure. Help me sleep."

"Get the man a beer," the white guy said to the black guy.

Justin felt the knotted muscles in the back of his neck and shoulders unwind at the white guy's change in tone. It was conciliatory, damned near friendly. Maybe by tomorrow, after a good night's sleep, he'd come up with an angle that would get him away from this pair.

34

The black guy remained in the kitchen, leaning on the counter, sipping a brew. The white guy returned to the table with two open bottles of Heineken. He held one across the table for Justin, who took it and drained half in one long pull. His throat was raw from talking and the foamy beer felt good going down, though it was a little bitter.

"Do you even own a Corvette?" the white guy asked.

"Like I'd drive a shitbox like that," Justin snorted. "I had a Ferrari for a while, but my accountant told me it was a little showy."

"Your accountant," the white guy said, running a finger down his written list. "Martin Best."

"Yep. Marty said the taxman might wonder how I was driving an Italian sportscar on under two hundred a year."

"You guys work with each other outside your little network here."

"Sure. Sure. We know each other. We can damned sure trust one another, am I right?"

"Like the Masons."

The white guy wasn't trying to be funny, but it struck Justin that way. He passed some beer through his nose, which only made him giggle more.

"The Masons," he said, waggling a hand at the white guy while he shook with laughter.

The white guy wasn't laughing, not even a smile.

"Woo, this beer's hittin' me," Justin said. "Must be my empty stomach."

The words were getting harder to say. His lips felt thick, and moving his tongue to speak was a chore. Keeping his eyes open was taking a great deal of effort too. He looked across the table at the white guy, who kept moving in and out of focus in a field of crimson. He could see a shadow against the lights from the kitchen behind him, the black guy stepping closer. Justin fought to keep his neck upright, his head listing to the right as though it was filling with sand.

"Masons," he slurred, drooling.

The red turned to black, then nothing.

———

"WHAT'D YOU GIVE HIM?" Levon said, looking across the table at the lawyer sitting slack-shouldered in the chair, his head lolled to one side and mouth hanging open.

"Little bit of everything," Wesley said. "Oxy. Paxil. Xanax. Got a shitload left over from what the VA sent me home with."

"That'll do it."

"So, we just kill him now?" Wesley sounded glum.

Levon nodded.

"While he's asleep?"

"That was your idea."

"That's cold."

"Is it? How'd you feel watching those videos?"

"I couldn't handle much of that shit. I mean, Jesus, one of them was a TV weatherman I used to watch up in Nashville."

Justin made a gagging sound. One of his legs was twitching in an arhythmic spasm. The beer bottle dropped from his trembling fingers and spilled on the floor.

"You'd have killed him then, wouldn't you? That weatherman. When you saw him doing what he was doing?" Levon asked.

"That's sick shit. This fucker is sick. Those poor damned kids." Wesley raised his beer to his lips, then changed his mind and dropped his hand.

"You think we should turn him over to the law? You think we do that, we're not the ones in trouble?" Levon asked.

"Man, what was *your* ROE?" Rules of Engagement.

"'Leave them where you find them' was my only directive."

"What unit were you with?"

"It didn't really have a name."

"Jesus." Wesley held the cool bottle to his forehead.

"What's the difference, bro?" Levon said. "What's the difference between this guy and the hadjis you ran into with their rentboys?"

"Buddy of mine was in Helmand. Said that shit was common as dirt there. Boys. Little girls. Sick shit. Don't make capping a man in cold blood easier."

"I don't think about it," Levon said. "Till I met you, I never talked about it."

"Lucky me," Wesley said with a weak smile.

"He's seizing," Levon said.

The lawyer's body convulsed, legs kicking, free arm flailing. His head bobbed back and forth, a dry strangled sound rattling in his throat. They watched while his body fought the rich mix of sedatives and antidepressants overloading his system. As though cued by a finger snap, his body went slack, the sudden weight of it tipping the chair to one side. He crashed to the floor, striking his head on the tile with a hollow crack. A few more spasms, and he lay still.

Wesley rounded the table to look at the sad heap of the man lying on the floor in a puddle of spilled beer. "He ain't breathing."

"Who gets to bury him?"

"Ground's frozen."

"You said you found some dynamite?" Levon reminded him.

35

"Who's Levon Cade?" Vince Holland said.

"He's trouble," Tony Marcoon said.

Laura Strand had returned to the office lent to them by the county, her battery recharged after a few hours' sleep. She called a meeting with Tony and Vince only. They were protected from the cold, drizzling rain by a covered portico behind the county building where they had been set up by Sheriff Meyers. The cold air was helping blow the cobwebs out of Laura's head. Tony took the opportunity for a smoke break, standing upwind.

She filled Vince in on Levon Cade, the man who had been the focus of a combined FBI/Treasury Department task force she and Tony had served on a few years back. Even a brief summation of Cade's life since his discharge from the USMC included a long list of federal crimes committed in the United States and abroad.

"And this guy's still walking around?" Vince said.

"He made a deal," Tony said.

"What kind of deal?"

"The kind the President signs."

"As in, 'of the United States?' So, he got pardoned?"

"Not exactly," Laura said. "More of a dispensation. Cade had something the government wanted. He traded it for full immunity."

"What kind of juice gets someone a pass for homicide, kidnapping, and interstate flight?" Vince wanted to know.

"He knew where some bodies were buried," Laura told them.

"Along with a few billion—that's with a 'B'—dollars Uncle Sam wanted back," Tony said.

"Okay. All sins forgiven," Vince said. "But he doesn't have a Get Out of Jail Free card, right? If he's our boy for these pattern murders, then he's used up his favors."

"Yeah. Tony and I have been here before. Cade is kind of radioactive."

"The chief of our task force?" Tony added. "They got her counting telephone poles in Idaho."

"Then we set up surveillance on this guy?" Vince said. "Seems a long way to go for what could be a coincidence. We have a case here, even if our suspect is AWOL. I mean, this congressman is the lead we should be following."

"You're not wrong," Laura said.

"We have a shit-ton of evidence to sift through, and we haven't even heard back on those hard drives or phones," Vince said. "Not for nothing, but I think this Cade guy is living in your heads rent-free."

"That could be true," Laura admitted.

"Still…" Tony let the word hang and took a last drag.

"It's worth a look," Laura said. "It might even give us a better angle of attack on this. We've stirred something up here. I go to get a warrant from a federal judge, and a few hours later, a congressman is telling our suspect to get out of Dodge?"

"This shit goes deep." Tony flipped his butt into some boxwoods growing against the building.

"Right. So maybe we can't go straight at this. Cade might just be the better way to get this done. If we like him for the killings, he might be a back door for us to build an unassailable case against some players we couldn't otherwise touch."

"This all sounds like a wish-list approach." Vince shook his head. "It's weak cheese."

"We can't do anything much until Quantico gets back to us," Laura said. "I say it's worth a day for one of us."

"You're the boss," Vince said with a shrug.

36

The dull thump from a single stick of buried dynamite echoed down the holler. It sounded like a massive door being shut.

A cloud of black starlings exploded from the trees into the pink overcast of the pre-dawn sky. The soil shuddered for a thousand yards all around. A slab of snow the size of a grand piano slid off the roof of the double-wide. The brush around the holler came alive with the thrashing of animals fleeing the unexpected thunder. The quiet afterward was profound and deep.

Wesley pulled the wires off the terminals and set the hand-crank detonator aside. A hundred yards away, he'd set the stick of RDX at the bottom of a six-foot hole augered into the icy ground. Now, a dome of dust, rocks, and dirt was settling over it.

Once the debris cloud began to clear, Levon said, "Let's see how we did." He made for the blast site, the tarp-wrapped corpse of the lawyer slung over his shoulder in a fireman's carry. Wesley followed with a couple of shovels and a bag of lime.

The dynamite had created a nearly round crater a

good six feet deep. Levon slung the body off his shoulder to fall to the floor of the hole. Wesley cut along the top of the lime sack with a clasp knife and emptied it over the body. They shoveled rocks and soil into the grave until it was roughly level. By spring, the cogonsgrass would cover it in an impenetrable carpet.

The sun was full up by the time they'd finished. They walked back to the shed.

"You know your way around explosives," Levon said. "That was as neat a job as I've ever seen."

"I had good instructors in demo school." Wesley took the shovel from Levon's hand to put it back in place inside the tool shed. "And it's surprising how exact you can be laying ordnance with no one shooting at you."

They returned to the double-wide, and neither man said anything until they sat down to a breakfast of scrambled eggs, sausage, fried potatoes, and hot coffee.

"Jesus, Levon," Wesley said. "A congressman?"

"Settle down. I have a rule," Levon said, digging a fork into a mound of eggs. "I don't shoot public officials above the county level."

Wesley looked up sharply to see if the other man was joking. He caught the slightest hint of a smile on Levon's face.

"Shit." Wesley shook his head.

"But I can't expect to put an end to this bunch, going at it the way I am."

"You have a new plan? Or do I blast some new holes for you?"

"I'm still sticking to my original objective. Make enough of a stink that they can't ignore it. A mess too big to cover up."

"Does that include bringing any more guests up here?"

"You remember my ROE?"

"'Leave 'em where you find 'em,' or something to that effect?"

"I think this Hacienda is the end game."

"Goin' down to Georgia." Wesley shook his head again and scooped up a mouthful of home fries smothered in ketchup.

"You wanna come with me?"

"You *trying* to get me in trouble? I thought we were starting to become friends."

"We're already friends, Wes. We buried a body together."

"Huh. Next, you'll be asking me to go golfing with you."

"I don't golf." Levon looked across the table at him. That trace of a smile again.

"Well, I don't go around killing white guys. Even if they are a pack of sick motherfuckers."

They ate in silence for a while. Wesley broke the quiet when Levon came back from taking his plate to the sink.

"He never told his side."

"Side?" Levon retook his seat and picked up his coffee mug.

"The lawyer never pled his own case. No apologies. No story to tell."

"What would he have said?"

"I don't know. 'I showed them love.' 'My uncle raped me, so I'm twisted that way.'" Wesley frowned into his breakfast. "Point is, he said nothing."

"Your mistake is in comparing him to yourself." Levon took a sip of coffee. "Men like that aren't the same as you or me. They're small inside. Empty. They need to fill that place with power over something. They abuse a child because they can, and that fills the emptiness and makes them feel like bigger men."

"It's not just that they're kinky?"

"It's got nothing to do with sex. They hurt these kids, and they know it. It's about hurting something that can't hurt you back."

"You have kids?"

"Two girls."

"That why you do this, Levon? To protect them?"

"My girls? Anyone ever tried to hurt them would find themselves in a very bad place."

"'Cause of you?"

"Naw. 'Cause of *them*."

"Can't wait to meet the family," Wesley said with a smirk. He stood to clear his plate.

37

An hour and a half drive north through freezing rain took Laura to Haley. It was after hours when she arrived, but the county sheriff agreed to see her at his home.

It was a modest rancher set well off a two-lane with two Re-Elect Elmo signs in the front yard. She'd seen a few of those signs on her trip through the mostly rural county. She pulled onto the concrete drive past a mailbox with STRUTHERS hand-painted on either side.

She parked her rental next to a 4WD with the county seal on its doors. The sheriff met her on the driveway. He was a late middle-aged man, still in his uniform khakis and tunic under a woolen coat. He wore a welcoming smile and held out an open umbrella for her. At his side, a rangy lop-eared hound stood wagging its tail.

"You must be Miss Strand," he said and nodded at the dog. "Don't mind Emily. She's my official greeter."

"Thanks for seeing me, Sheriff," Laura said as they shook hands.

"I could have met you at the office. Is this official business? You didn't tell my secretary what this is about."

"Let's call it exploratory, just for now," she said and followed him into the house under the shelter of the shared umbrella.

Inside, she was introduced to Marjorie Struthers, the sheriff's wife, who offered up a plate of homemade Christmas cookies and hot tea. Laura was chilled from her short walk to the house and accepted both with appreciation. Though less than seventy miles north of Huntsville, it was appreciably colder in this county's higher elevation. There were still patches and drifts of snow on the ground.

The sheriff showed her out onto a porch at the back of the house that was enclosed by unadorned windows in a wood frame. The dog followed them in and took up her place on a tartan dog bed by a ceramic stove. The stove took the chill from the air. The glass panes were streaked with condensation. A Christmas tree stood in another corner, and there was a laundry basket of toys by it.

"Grandchildren?" Laura took a seat in a wicker chair after the sheriff had cleared it of a few magazines lying on the seat.

"Two. Boy and girl. My daughter's. Marjorie helps out sitting them most days." Elmo Struthers took what was obviously his accustomed chair, a well-worn leather recliner. "Now, what brings a US marshal to the backwoods on a nasty night like this?"

"You had a case earlier in the year," she said. "It involved multiple homicides and some missing children."

The sheriff's accommodating smile faded, first from his eyes and then his lips. The change added ten years to his appearance.

"You mean the Sherwood thing."

"Daniel Sherwood? That was one of the adult victims. The house was in his name, am I right?"

"It was. His mother's name, actually, only she's long deceased."

The sheriff looked past her to where his wife was entering the porch with a plate of cookies and a steaming mug of Lipton for Laura. After thank yous and you're welcomes, Marjorie Struthers vanished back into the house to leave the law officers to their business.

"What's your interest here, Marshal?" He'd dispensed with calling her Miss.

"You had three adult males found dead at the house. Several minor children were found at the house who'd been on the missing list, and the bodies of more missing children were discovered buried in a crawlspace under the house."

"That's about the size of it. We found the remains of more than two dozen kids, all boys, under there. We were able to link most of them to missing cases here and in neighboring counties. A few of them are still unidentified."

"And the three adult males?"

"Sherwood and two others. One of them was a registered sex offender. You know, I…" Elmo's voice trailed off, and he looked at the hound in the dog bed, kicking her paws in a dream.

Laura gave him time by taking a sip from her mug.

"Look, there's part of it you don't know," he said. "There were two more bodies there that night, a Georgia state representative from Smyrna and his state police bodyguard."

"A politician and a cop were killed? By the same actors?"

"It looked that way to us. That's how we were treating it till state CID took it off us and locked us out. Next, I heard the pair from Georgia had died in a single-car accident somewhere over the Georgia line. Had to hear about that on the TV news."

"You eye-deed the state rep that night?"

"No. That was me puttin' two and two together after the fact. We positive eye-deed the statie from the badge we found on him. That's before the detectives up from Montgomery confiscated all our evidence. Once I saw the story on the news, I knew my job was to keep my mouth shut."

"How did you feel about that?"

Elmo shrugged. "No matter what story was told, the sumbitch was dead. He was gonna have to answer to Jesus."

"The boys that were rescued. Did any of them share what happened at the house?"

"Not much. They were traumatized, you understand. Or do I have to tell you what that house was all about?" The pain of the memories was plainly etched on the sheriff's face.

"I do understand, sir. We believe it ties into a case we're pursuing in the Huntsville area."

Laura filled him in with as much as he needed to know about the multi-state pedophile network they'd uncovered and the similarities with the case here in this county. Also, the matter of their missing suspect and, once again, a bodyguard murdered in the process.

He nodded. "I see where you might think there's a connection there."

"What were your theories on the killings at the Sherwood house?"

"A falling out, mostly. Dads Sherwood was the kind of guy to make enemies. A bully, you see. We thought maybe he'd crossed the wrong fella over money or like that. A bully always meets a bigger bully one day. Way of the world. Karma."

"Do any of the rescued children still live in the area?"

"I know of two that do." He leaned forward to look at her with eyes bordering on pleading. "You don't plan on questioning any of them, do you?"

"It might come to that, sir," she said. "I'll do my best to avoid it."

"I'd appreciate that."

"I do have another question," she said, picking up the mug of tea. "How did this case not get national attention? Missing children. All the evidence of a serial killer. You did call in state CID on it. You say there was a coverup, but the information had to have gone public."

"Something you'll find out about mountain folks, Marshal, especially if you keep on looking into this matter. We tend to keep to ourselves up in here, and don't nobody outside care much about some missing white trash or colored boys. No offense meant."

"None taken."

"Call it a code. Call it mountain pride. But something as shameful and pure-D damned *evil* as this happens, we deal with it and put it behind us. No one up here's anxious to have the world looking at the worst of us and passing judgment."

And dead men tell no tales, Laura thought.

"I can see how you kept it out of the media," Laura said. And she could. The news cycles that ignored thousands of murders every year in the inner cities would have had little interest in the abductions and murders of some kids in some backwoods county.

"As I told your secretary, I'm part of a Missing Children Unit with the marshal service," she continued. "What I really don't understand is how this didn't register with any federal agencies. I mean, I only heard about this case earlier today."

"Well, we had a little help with that from Montgomery. Someone ran interference to let the state boys handle it all," the sheriff said, helping himself to a cookie from the plate between them—a green-iced Christmas tree dappled with powdered sugar snow.

"Who was that, sir?"

"A congressman. Phil Barnes."

38

"He don't want to talk to you," Carline Loomis said.

"I'd like to hear that from him," Laura said.

Russell Loomis' mother had come out of the trailer she shared with her son to meet Laura when she pulled up next to a ten-year-old Kia parked on the gravel drive. The woman, not much taller than Laura, held a hastily donned cardigan tightly around her. She stood by Laura's rental, eyes hard, chin up, and jaw set for a fight. Laura stepped from the car and held up her badge and ID. The woman wouldn't look at it. Instead, she fixed her baleful stare on Laura.

"You're hearing it from me, and I'm his mother. And that's all you need to hear."

Laura looked past the woman standing sentry, arms folded. The trailer she and her son called home was old but well-maintained. A partly deflated Santa sat at the foot of steps that led to a narrow wooden deck. Visible through the glass of the storm door was a wreath frosted with faux snow hanging on the front door. She thought she saw the curtain move in one of the front windows. She couldn't be sure.

"I have no interest here in making your son relive his experiences," Laura said in her best accommodating voice. "I only have a few questions about the night he was rescued. Specifically, what and who he might have seen."

"He told all that to the police. Told 'em over and over. You need to leave him and the other boys alone. Let them forget all that." Carline's eyes gleamed with the beginning of tears.

"I've read the official reports, Mrs. Loomis, but that's not the whole story." The evening before, Laura had had the CID files sent to her official email. She'd read them in her room at a Budget Inn in nearby Haley. The paperwork had been maddening in its vagueness, and much of the information was redacted or sealed since the case involved juvenile victims.

"That's all the story you're gonna hear."

"Russell told about how he was rescued. I wanted to know about the man who did that. What he looked like. Anything he might have said that—"

"You leave those men alone!" Carline shouted, knuckles white where she clutched the sweater against her. "Those men are saints! They were angels sent from heaven!"

Men. More than one man.

"He told you about them?" Laura asked.

"All I need to know! And now, you know all I'm gonna tell you." Carline tilted her head to the right in a farewell gesture before turning back to the trailer.

Laura watched the woman stomp onto the deck and into the double-wide with a slam of the storm door that made the aluminum frame hum. Somewhere out of sight, a dog started barking. The curtain she thought she'd seen move remained parted, a sliver of dark in the gap.

She drove out of the subdivision of trailers and pre-fabs to a Shell station. She got a hot coffee in the food mart and sipped it as she topped off the tank of her rental. Leaning against the side of the sedan, she watched a big semi rumble along the county road the station fronted on. It carried a monster combine chained down on a flatbed. A pickup flying wide-load flags raced ahead of it.

Across the lot, three men were in animated conversation in front of an SUV with a fresh deer carcass tied across the hood. The pump handle clunked full in her hand, and she lifted it to replace it in the holster. She pressed Yes for a receipt before turning to get back into her car.

From the direction she'd just come, a boy coasted on a bike into the station lot. He climbed off and walked toward her, one hand on a handlebar to roll the bike beside him. The bike looked new. A Christmas gift, perhaps. Laura was no judge of kids' ages, but she guessed he was older than twelve. He had blue eyes she thought she had seen before. She certainly recognized the sadness in them.

"You were talkin' to my mom," the boy said by way of an introduction.

"Russell?"

"Call me Russ."

"Would you like to get in my car to talk? It's warmer."

The boy shook his head.

"You have something you wanted to tell me, Russ?" She came around the front of the car.

"Those men. You asked my mom about those men."

"How many men were there?"

"Two."

"What kind of men were they?"

"White men. One of 'em was shot."

"Did they say anything to you? Did they use their names?"

"He told us we were brave. The bigger one. The one wasn't shot."

"When did he say this?"

"After we helped him load up his truck."

Laura took a step closer. Russell Loomis flinched at her approach, and she stopped.

"What did you load into his truck, Russ?" she asked, tamping down the urge to press harder.

"It was old videotapes like I seen at my grandpa's house. Boxes of 'em in a room that was always locked." His eyes shifted away, seeing that house again, the memories returning in flashes.

"Like movies?"

"Naw. They all had labels someone wrote on."

"And the man, the big man, wanted them?"

"Yes, ma'am. Then he told us he couldn't stay but for us to call the police and stay on the line so's they could find us."

"What else did he say, Russ?"

"That he'd like if we didn't talk about him to no one. Only he told us not to lie if we didn't feel like it was right."

"And did you ever tell anyone, Russ?"

"No one but my mom. No one till I'm tellin' you."

"Thank you, Russ. The man was right. You're very brave."

"I don't feel brave." Russell threw a leg over his bike. "Mostly, I just feel scared all the time."

She leaned on the rental to watch him ride away, standing on the pedals to climb the inclining road away from the Shell station until he was gone up the slope and behind the trees.

39

The house was a rambling two-story wood-frame deal, a farmhouse of the kind that'd had extensions put on as the family grew in size. The exterior walls were covered in green shakes that were probably asbestos. Behind the house was some kind of machine barn for farm equipment.

Laura pulled up to the front door and stepped out of the rental. The door was wide open. Tatters of sagging police tape made a riffling sound when the wind off the open fields caused them to flutter.

She tried to call her unit to tell them where she was, but her phone had zero bars. Not a big surprise. She'd driven through a gauntlet of steep ridges to get here. This place wasn't even locatable on her GPS service. The only way she'd found it was by asking questions at a couple of houses along the county road.

She stepped onto the front porch and heard a scuttling sound from within the darkness beyond the open doorway. She pulled her sidearm, chambered a round, and called, "Anyone there?"

A pair of raccoons raced out of the darkness. They

scrambled under the bottom bar of the porch railing and away into the weeds growing all around the house.

Laura had never seen a raccoon outside of television commercials. She'd never realized how big they could be. In the back of her mind, she recalled reading somewhere that nearly every raccoon was a rabies carrier. She kept her Sig in her hand as she aimed the beam of a Maglite into the gloomy interior.

The house smelled of rancid grease and nicotine. She was in a long hallway that led to the back. She found what she believed was the room described by Russell Loomis. There was a row of hasps for deadbolt locks bolted along the frame. The door was leaning on its side against a wall. The hinges had been blown off by what looked like shotgun blasts. Deep gouges scored the jamb.

Inside the windowless room, the walls were lined with shelves, all empty. A stout safe sat open on the floor, the door and top still greasy with the residue of finger-print powder. Evidence of the state detectives' investigation was everywhere. Circles in chalk around dark splotches on the faded oak floorboard. Blood from the "one was shot" that Russell had told her about.

She explored the rest of the house, wary of possible fur-bearing squatters. More unsettling than the prospect of rabid raccoons was the nature of the house. The presence of children's toys and decorations in a house that was so obviously occupied only by men told a story Laura preferred not to dwell on. With her phone, she snapped pictures of anything she thought might be relevant.

Every door on the second floor was equipped with security locks that bolted from the outside. Every room had wrought iron bars outside the windows. Most of the doors showed wear on the inside, scratches or gouges as if the occupants had tried to get out. Each room was furnished with mismatched pieces that looked third-hand. Many of the rooms had wallpaper with childish themes of saccharine clowns or insipid nursery rhymes.

There were more signs of recent violence in evidence. Blood on the walls and carpet of a hallway and a bathroom that looked like an abattoir, the linoleum floor black with dried blood. More blood on a staircase, and bullet and shot holes in the plaster.

Cables ran from holes in the walls along the top of the crown molding in the hallways. The cables were stapled in place and painted over to disguise them. They ran from each room, and it didn't take long to find the lenses of video cameras hidden in the upper corners of each room as well as some artfully concealed in the designs of the various wallpapers. She tracked the cables as they merged and conjoined to run downstairs, where they terminated at a wooden cabinet where three VCRs, all crusted with fingerprint powder, sat in a TV room.

It wasn't until she got back to Haley that she stopped to call Tony Marcoon. She parked in the lot of a place that looked like it had once been a Hardee's but was now called John John's Chicken Pit. The smell of barbecue through the closed windows of the rental was making her mouth water. She was definitely giving this place a try once she hung up.

"I'm sending you the pictures I took," she said and tapped her screen to attach the most recent file.

"Check your texts." Tony's voice from the dash speakers. "I sent on those unredacted case files for you."

"From the multiple homicide?"

"That's the one. I had to throw a serious scare into some wonk down there. Hope I scared him enough not to file a report."

"You make unauthorized threats?"

"I might have stretched the truth a little. I might have mentioned Homeland Security."

"Tony, you are one in a million."

"You heading back soon? We're promised something off those hard drives before end of business."

"I'll be back by then," she said, glancing at the smiling cartoon chicken bidding her welcome by the front door of John John's. Best BBQ in Bama, the chicken promised.

"I only have one more stop to make after I grab some lunch," Laura added before signing off.

———

"A GOOD STEAM cleaning and a coat of paint, and this place'll do just fine," Fern said, walking the interior of the garage building.

"You have plans for these?" Levon nodded at two hydraulic lifts bolted to the floor in mechanics' bays.

"Find someone to haul 'em outta here for scrap. Maybe someone'll even want to buy 'em." Fern turned to Josh Rimes, the current owner of the property. Josh's dad and granddad had run Rimes Auto Service for decades. Josh worked for a Ford dealership in Haley and had no interest in owning his own repair business.

"Could be." Josh raised his shoulders. "I can ask around. Maybe take some pictures and put 'em on Facebook or Craig's."

"Plenty of room to get three thumpers going." Fern gestured, placing imaginary vats across the shop floor. "We run a gas line in here. There's room for a bottling machine and label station. We can label and bottle by hand at first. You know, till enough regular orders come in."

"You'll need to hire some help." Levon scraped the sole of his boot across the cracked concrete floor. It was stained black in places from years of oil changes. "And this floor needs resurfacing and tile if you're gonna pass code."

"How close are y'all to getting' your financing?" Josh asked.

"You're not about to hand me some bullshit about other buyers now, are you, Josh?" Fern said.

Josh looked away. "Just askin'."

"We won't hear till the new year," Fern said. "What with the holidays and all."

"But y'all think it'll go through?" Josh looked from Fern to Levon.

"Tell you what," Levon took out his wallet and counted out some bills. "Here's five hundred now. We'll call it earnest money. That suit you, Josh?"

They shook on it, and Josh left them with wishes for good luck in their whiskey business.

"You really think we can make a go of this, Levon?" Fern asked as they drove out of Colby.

"There's no 'we' about it," Levon answered. He made the turn onto the county road. "You're running the day to day."

"I thought this might be a family business," Fern grumbled and looked out the window at the passing trees and mailboxes.

"And don't even think of involving Merry and Hope. You know they can't work at a still at their age."

"Merry said she'd help me design the Blue Moon website."

"Long as she does it from home."

"That's okay. Alma's got a nephew just got laid off at Nissan. He's looking for work." Alma was the wife of Wendell Cade, Fern's only surviving sibling.

"So, it's still a family business. With me as a silent partner."

The Avalanche climbed a switchback lined along one side with the brow of a sheer granite face where the cut had been made for the grading long ago. Pines rose above the rock ledge on up the steep incline that formed one wall of the holler they called home. A rusted steel guard rail with several sections missing ran along the left side of the road. On the other side of the intermittent rail, the ground fell away sharply into a dark ravine, the floor hidden by pine tops wavering in the wind.

"Do you think it'll go?" Fern turned to look at his nephew.

"It's got as good a chance as any." Levon shrugged. "Besides, it only has to look like a success on paper."

"That's so. Only I'd like it to stand on its own two feet."

"Well, either way, you're getting to spin that wheel." Levon turned onto the gravel of their driveway past the rusted mailbox with no name on it.

"Who's this?" Fern said.

A Buick Regal neither of them recognized was pulled up to the house. Rascal leapt at the driver's side door, yapping away while Bella circled the car, tail wagging. The driver appeared to be alone.

40

An older man climbed out of the Avalanche cab and called off the dogs. She recalled him from the last time she was here. A taller, younger man in work clothes and a barn coat approached the driver's side of the Buick, hands at his sides. She'd only ever seen photos of him from twenty years ago.

The pair of dogs turned their attention from the strange car to rush up to their returning masters, the hound at a lazy lope and the terrier as if launched by a rocket.

Laura Strand got out of the car and held up a badge and ID.

"Laura Strand, marshal service," she said. "Are you Levon Cade?"

"That's me." He stopped four paces away to stand waiting on the gravel.

"Is there someplace we could talk?" She watched the older man shooing the dogs into the house and following them inside.

"Here's fine."

"It's kind of cold." The temperature had fallen, and

the wind was gusting down off the wooded ridge that rose behind the stable. The afternoon sun did nothing to reduce the chill.

"Then make it fast."

"It would be better for you if you cooperated."

Levon was silent for a moment, looking past her at the open field and the woods beyond the house. She was about to repeat herself when he held up a hand, eyes still focused on some distant point.

"The last time the marshals were here, they arrested my uncle and took my little girl away. Put her in foster care. Now, you'll excuse me if I'm not making an effort to make you feel welcome here. And you folks never come one at a time if you mean business. That means you're not here to take me in. Say what you have to say. Then leave me be."

"All right then," she said. "We can talk here."

Laura realized the man was doing everything he could to tamp down anger and keep his voice calm and even. She was also very much aware that she was in the back of beyond in a place where people had rules all their own and not much use for federal agents. She hadn't told Tony where she was going after lunch. There was never a moment in her life she could recall when she'd felt as isolated as she did at this moment.

"I'm working with the new Missing Children Unit of the marshals. We're looking into a network of traffickers, and some of our investigations have leads to suspects in Huntsville. We heard of a recent multiple homicide case here in this county. It involved some men who were holding abducted minors for the purpose of prostitution."

"What's that got to do with me?"

Laura was ready for that question. She'd read the case files Tony'd sent her on her phone. The redactions were gone, and the sealed portions were now open to her. She'd read the full reports from both the county and the state CID detectives. These included the final report from the state medical examiner who'd positively identified the remains of eighteen minors, all male, with eight more too badly decomposed for a confident analysis, all interred in trash bags under the dirt floor beneath the Sherwood house.

"One of the bodies they found under the house was eye-deed as Trevor Cade. He lived in Haley until he disappeared a few months ago. Is he a relation?"

"He was the son of one of my cousins," Levon said. "I never knew the boy."

"The investigation into the scene of the murder found a graveyard full of children ages five through twelve in the crawlspace under the house. There was also evidence of further crimes removed from the house."

"I heard about it. Went to the boy's funeral. His mother lived here in the county. She's moved on now."

"And your cousin, Edward Lee Cade, the boy's father. Have you seen him recently?"

"Haven't seen Teddy since we were kids. Since high school."

"If you did know something, would you share the information with me?"

"Have a safe drive out of here, Marshal Strand," Levon said and walked past her to the porch steps.

She waited until he was inside the house before climbing into her rental. That asshole terrier had scratched the paint on the door with its claws. She pulled her gloves off stiff fingers to hold her hands against the vents in the dash, the heater turned to MAX.

Cade was stonewalling; that was for damn sure. It might be that he knew more than he'd say. It might just as well be a deep resentment at the raw treatment his family had received from the task force headed up by Nancy Valdez that she used to belong to. If that was the case, Laura felt his reaction was justified. Valdez had pushed that investigation into Cade's alleged criminal actions to the very edge of legality and over into open harassment. Add that history to the natural inclination of Appalachians to be suspect of the US government, and Cade's attitude was understandable.

Still, there was Cade's undeniable link to the murders at the Sherwood house, though maybe a second cousin he'd never met wasn't that much of a link. Maybe blood didn't run that deep around here? Could family bonds be strong enough to unleash vigilante justice for relations distant enough to be strangers? Then again, these were people who, not that long ago, had lived by the feud, and taking the law into their own hands was how things were done around here. They'd only located Cade the first time by sending in one of their own, a former Alabama local, on an undercover canvass. It had been like sending a spy into a foreign country.

She sat for a while longer, watching the house and allowing the heat to take the ache from her hands before backing up on the gravel and turning the rental around. It was just past two but already looking like dusk as the winter sun sank behind a ridgeline.

On her way back down to the snaky access road, she saw a pair of riders on horseback coming out of the trees. Laura slowed down. The riders reined in on the grass beside the gravel drive to watch her trundle by. She gave them a professional smile in passing. Two girls in heavy parkas, hoods up, and heads encased in woolen hats. The horses blew clouds of vapor and stamped as the strange car rolled by.

The smaller of the girls, dark hair poking out from

under her cap, offered more of a wince than a smile. The
older girl did not try to return Laura's smile. She studied
the unknown car and its driver with the same look of
cold appraisal Laura had seen in Cade's eyes.

The older girl was Meredith Cade, Levon Cade's
daughter. Laura turned away then, unable to meet the
girl's steady gaze.

41

"Who was that?" Merry asked.

"Your uncle is making hot chocolate for you and Hopey," Levon said. At the kitchen table, he feigned interest in a six-month-old issue of *American Hunter*.

"Don't change the subject." Merry stood just inside the kitchen doorway, careful to keep her muddy riding boots on the doormat. Rascal had joined her on the porch, pawing at her leg for attention.

"You leave your sister to put the horses up?"

"I helped her crosstie them. I'll go back to help her once you tell me who that was."

"Some lady who got lost."

"Nobody's ever gotten that lost, ever."

"She was a census taker."

"Is that so, Uncle Fern?"

"Don't get me in the middle of this." Fern made himself busy at the counter pouring milk into a pot.

"It's not a census year," Merry said.

"This lady's getting an early start," Levon said, pretending to read an article on caribou hunting in Alaska. "You're letting the heat out."

Merry gave him a narrowed-eyed look before slamming the door and marching back to the stable. The terrier bounded ahead of her.

"She's just worried about you," Fern said, putting the pot on the stovetop and setting the heat to medium. "So am I. What'd that woman want?"

"Just asked me some questions about something that had nothing to do with me."

"She's a revenue agent."

"Her badge said she's a marshal."

"Same difference. They're both Treasury. She's been here before."

Levon turned in his chair.

"When?"

"When they arrested me. She was one of the bunch took me outta here like a damned criminal." Fern rooted through the cabinets to retrieve a tin of cocoa powder.

"Is she the one who took Merry?"

"She was with them, but not the one in charge." Fern scooped spoonfuls of powder into the simmering pot. "*That* woman was a cast-iron bitch. You gonna tell me what the marshals want with you?"

"It wasn't the marshals. It was just her fishing around."

"About what?"

"Teddy Lee's boy."

"Shit, Levon." Fern took a seat across the table from his nephew.

"We're gonna have to get used to government types visiting now and then. Given my history, they're gonna think anything that happens for a hundred miles around here might be me."

"They don't have nothing?"

"And they're not gonna get anything. You're scorching the milk."

"Damn!" Fern leapt up to rescue his cocoa. It was bubbling over the sides of the pot. He lifted it off the flame and turned the dial to low before returning to the table.

"Merry has a right to worry over you. Jessie too."

"What's Jessie have to do with this?"

"She come by looking for you. Thinks maybe you're up to something."

"What'd you say to her?"

"I told her you just get yourself in a way now and then, but I damn sure know you *are* up to something. Late nights, whole days away, and locking yourself away in the shed for hours. And you didn't even come home the other night."

"You don't want to know."

"You're right. I'm ignorant and want to stay that way. Only whatever it is you're into, you need to remember you have two children counting on you and a woman who's stupid enough to maybe be in love with you. Is what you got going on worth risking that?"

"You're the one asked me to help Teddy Lee look for Trevor."

"And you found him. It's goddamn sad what happened, but you done that. You kept that promise. It's done."

"It's not."

"I don't know what you found looking for Trevor, and God knows, I don't want to know. I have enough shitty memories of my own to last me the rest of my life. These are your kids, Levon. You need to look out for what's your own."

"I can't walk away." Levon pushed away from the table. "And you can't ask me to."

Fern shifted in his chair to watch Levon leave the kitchen. He heard his nephew's steps on the stairs and looked at the bluetick hound regarding him with sad eyes. The dog's tail flicked against the wall, pleased to have Fern's attention.

"What are we gonna do with him, Bella?"

42

When Laura got back to their borrowed office, there were two men there she did not know.

"Laura, this is Agent Walsh and Agent Walker," Tony said, rising from behind his desk.

He didn't differentiate between the two, and it wouldn't have done her any good if he had. Both FBI men looked like they came out of the same mold: matching haircuts and suits bought off the same rack. They were here on business. There were cardboard cartons already sealed with evidence tape resting on a desk. One of the agents held out an open folder of documents.

"Marshal Strand? Good to meet you," either Walsh or Walker said to her, laying the folder on the desk and offering her a pen. "We need you to sign off on these AO 187s and these USM forms confirming the transfer of evidence into Bureau custody."

Well, good afternoon to you too, assholes, she thought as she took the forms and sat down to read through them.

"We'll need any notes you've taken as well," said either Walker or Walsh.

"Reading," she said. She heard Tony suppress a snort. At least *he* was enjoying this.

"Where were you since yesterday, Marshal?" Walsh or Walker said. "Marshal Marcoon said you went off the reservation."

"I said she was on a canvass, Agent," Marcoon said. "And I'm not a sworn-in marshal. I'm a Treasury agent on temporary assignment."

"What did this canvass deal with?" Walker or Walsh said.

"It was a dead-end. What aspect of this case is the Bureau taking on?" She made it a point to refuse the offer of a pen to take her Montblanc, a gift from her father, out of the pocket of her jacket.

"All of it." It was Walsh or Walker's turn. "You have multiple homicides that might be serial killings. Human trafficking and kidnapping. All interstate. Technically, this should never have been a case for your cowboys."

"We'll need your notes from the start of the case onwards," the other one put in. "Including yesterday and today."

She dug into a jacket pocket and produced her notebook, slipped the pad from the monogrammed kidskin cover, also a gift from her father, and handed over the pad. Her meetings with Sheriff Struthers and Carline Loomis were in there, with much of what the sheriff told her left out. There was no record of her meets with Russell Loomis or Levon Cade. She'd been driving a rental instead of a federal car, so there'd be no GPS record for them to check.

Walker or Walsh picked up the notebook pages with the disdain he might have shown while removing a dead mouse from a trap. He dropped the pages into an envelope and slapped a strip of red evidence tape over the flap before scribbling his signature and the date on the tape using the pen he'd offered Laura.

"How did you hear about this case?" Laura asked. "Our department has not submitted anything to the DOJ."

"The deputy director got a heads-up and sent us down here to bat cleanup," one of the agents said.

A certain congressman has been working the phone, Laura thought.

"Well, good luck with the case, Agents." Her smile wished them well while her eyes told them to go fuck each other.

"I'm sure we'll make some progress on the start you made," Walker or Walsh said by way of a farewell, and with cardboard cartons and folders in their arms, they left the room.

"And there they go," Tony said, rising from where he'd been sitting hipshot on the corner of a desk. "Off to slow-walk our case into eternity."

"Is it too early to go get a drink?" Laura folded her empty notebook cover and replaced it in her pocket.

"I'll call in Vince and the monster squad." Tony grinned. "We'll make a night of it."

———

THEY FOUND a place called Smokey's. It had a pool hall, and the music wasn't too loud. It was just down-market enough that there wouldn't be any cops there. A blue-collar, no-collar, drinking man's bar. The marshals took a table at the back and ordered pitchers.

"What were you thinking, boss?" Tony asked as he poured Laura a glass.

"I'm not sure. One-stop shopping?" She shrugged,

still unsure about her encounter with Levon Cade. She took the cool glass.

"Like he'd tie the case up with a bow?" Tony asked.

"Maybe I just wanted to read him, see if he was still on the game."

"And?"

"The man's a sphinx."

"You see this Cade for our baby-raper killer?" Bo Charles asked, looking up from a greasy menu card that promised Bama's Biggest Burgers.

"It's in his wheelhouse," Laura said.

"I like this guy already," Mountain remarked, snatching the menu out of Bo Charles' hand. "Taking too long."

"What's next?" Vince asked.

"We head home. Get new assignments." Laura took a sip. She hated beer but owed it to the guys to indulge.

"I mean, in this case," Vice said.

"That's the Bureau's problem now," she said.

"The feebs will go back to Quantico and rub their chins and scratch their heads and look at this case from the ass-end the way lawyers do," Tony said. "Then they'll chop it into slices because they're not big-picture thinkers. They'll hand the murders over to the geniuses at VICAP, who'll fuss over it until they decide they're looking for a white one-eyed, bed-wetting mama's boy of average height and weight who hates his daddy. And the rest of it, with help from friends in low places, will get buried under a truckload of Bureau bullshit."

"What happens to us?" Rizzo, Matt Rizzolli, asked.

"We go back to following around cattle farmers in Idaho, looking for one of those right-wing militias the director seems to think are everywhere." Vince drained his first glass.

"Fuck" was Spaz's, Vernon Spitz's, only contribution to the exchange.

"Pack your woolies," Tony said. "I have six months till I have my thirty in."

"What about you, Laura? You gonna go through any doors with us?" Vince asked.

"I've seen enough of the wicked world," she said, suddenly feeling tired. "I'm putting in for a transfer back to IRS. At least numbers make sense."

"Well, just remember your old pals if we ever come up for audit." Bo Charles raised his beer.

"I won't leave you a pot to piss in," she said and clinked glasses with him.

43

Brillings, Georgia had always been a sleepy little town, and in recent years, it had grown almost comatose.

The town had once been home to a textile mill with a defense department contract to produce material for military use. The big mill along Willard Creek had turned out cotton, wool, and denim for dress uniforms, fatigues, caps, webbing, and tents from the Great War of 1917 until the end of the Vietnam conflict. That contract had run out in the '80s, and with it, the regular infusion of federal dollars.

The population of Brillings had been halved by the turn of the millennium. Those remaining were mostly retirees, die-hards, or folks willing to make the one-hour commute to jobs at Raytheon or the Pepsi bottling plant in Albany in exchange for cheaper housing.

Late in the afternoon of a weekday, Levon turned off 82 south and drove for twenty minutes along a county road before hitting the main street of Brillings. It had probably once been a nice little town to grow up in. Now the business district, occupying two blocks of Main Street, was mostly boarded up. What were once a furniture store, a jewelry emporium, and a television and radio repair shop had whitewashed windows and FOR LEASE signs in the windows. Even the First Georgia Bank had long ago been shuttered. A gun and pawn shop was still in business, as was a pokey little corner drug store and a one-time 7-Eleven now renamed Daisy's Drive-U with handprinted signs in the window offering "Vaping Supplys." There was some effort to decorate for the season, with strands of faded tinsel hanging from some storefronts and an inflated snowman sagging atop the pawn shop's awning.

West of town, past a quarter-mile stretch of single homes, he crossed train tracks, followed by the intersection with the township road. He hooked a right and headed north. Sacajawea Road. There was no traffic, and he was able to take it slow and study both sides of the road. There were a few blocks of neatly spaced single homes and duplexes that gave way to larger lots with mobile homes and shotgun shacks on them. Then the road veered to the northwest, paralleling a shallow turn in the rail tracks. The tree line came to the road verge for long stretches, with gaps in the elms and mature oaks through which he could see older houses set back on deep lots.

He'd found the house he believed to be the Hacienda in a Google map search. He'd driven this road before virtually using the 3D feature. Seeing the house from the ground confirmed it: a big square saltbox of a house situated at the rear of a four-acre lot. He spotted the red shake siding through the row of hedges growing alongside the road behind a stacked stone knee wall that spanned the entire frontage of the property. An opening in the wall was the start of a hundred-yard driveway of crushed stone that led straight as a string to the house across an open lot of mown grass, now brown under the winter sun.

Levon took in all that in the seconds it took to pass the house. He drove on without slowing to follow the township road wherever it took him. It brought him to an east-west road called Goose Hollow Drive, and he turned right to take it east.

Goose Hollow continued for a mile or so before coming to an intersection with the rail tracks. He slowed the Avalanche to turn onto a rutted, gravel service road that ran alongside the tracks. It was weed-choked and poorly maintained but easily passable for the 4X4. He took it slow so as not to kick up more dust than was necessary.

Within ten minutes, he was behind the red house. He pulled the truck into the shadow of some sumac growing along the roadway. The house stood on the other side of the tracks. Another hundred yards of cleared ground ran from the tracks to the cyclone fence at the back of the property. The rail tracks ran along a sunken grade topped on this side by scrub pines and more sumac. From his position, he could see the back of the red house but would be invisible to anyone looking this way from there.

He stepped out of the cab and climbed onto the hardtop tonneau cover for a better perch. With a 30X scope, he scanned the house. A long row of cinder-block garage-like buildings blocked his view of the first floor, but he knew from studying satellite images that the backyard had either been graveled or paved for use as a parking area. On the sat images, only a small patch of grass remained in the yard with what looked to be a swing set. There was room behind the house to park twenty cars or more, not counting whatever available space was in the garages.

Nothing changed during his long examination of the house and the surrounding properties. The nearest houses were an acre or more away. It was late afternoon, and the only movement he saw was a mob of crows working their way from one leafless tree to another.

The house was unremarkable except for the presence of bars across the second-floor windows. They appeared to be wrought iron, and each covered only the lower sash of each window. Someone inside could open the window for air but not climb through. The upper sashes were uncovered but were probably nailed or screwed into place.

Like the Sherwood house, this place had never been on the market. His visits to various real estate sites had given Levon nothing to work with. No interior photos or schematics. He'd be going in blind, though he could safely assume the rooms with the barred windows were cells for any captive children on the premises.

The county tax rolls had told him the home belonged to a Mr. Edward James Dutton and had done so since 1995 when he'd inherited it from his parents. Ma and Pa Dutton appeared to have been the only other owners, having built the house in 1967. There were no liens or encumbrances, and Ed Dutton paid his property taxes on time each year.

From his vantage point, Levon saw two rear entrances: a Dutch door atop a set of wooden steps that probably opened into the kitchen and a slanted steel Bilco door leading to a basement. The Bilco had a chain and a stout padlock run through the door handles. There was no way to exit the basement from inside. There was a double-door entrance at the front of the house, and a wood-railed porch ran across the front exposure.

He looked for any other details. There were motion lights mounted under the eaves and above the rear door.

He saw no sign of video cameras. The garage had a series of windows across the back, and he could see sunlight through a few of them. That meant the doors were open. He saw little of interest except for the swings, a rusty set of rainbow-colored steel tubing, the grass worn to bare dirt beneath each of the three seats from years of kids dragging their feet on the ground.

Satisfied he'd seen all he needed to of the house, he scanned the surrounding country. Each of the neighboring houses had deep lots that ended at the rail grade. On his side of the tracks, he could see open land through the thin screen of sumacs and pines that grew along the tracks. They looked like fields left fallow for the winter. Here and there, a streak of unmelted snow lay in a furrow. Over the slope of a hill to the north, he saw the tops of a row of silos.

There was little chance of his being seen by anyone since the Avalanche was pulled well into the sumacs. From his vantage point, he could watch the house by night to get a sense of the activity there. He'd sleep on the rear seat of the truck tonight. The nearest motel was a forty-five-minute drive away. Now that he was onsite, he wanted to stay here, and there was nothing to be gained by checking into a motel other than added exposure. No one had seen or would remember him coming into town. He preferred to keep it that way.

44

As night fell, Levon watched Christmas lights flicker on across the fronts of houses along Sacajawea. Atop the roof of the home off to the right of the Hacienda, a sleigh and some reindeer blinked to life. The back of the Hacienda remained dark. He couldn't tell if there were lights strung at the front.

Once it was full dark, a bright white source of light came on in front of and to one side of the house to illuminate the driveway. Watching through binoculars from the bed of the truck, Levon scanned the house and yard for movement. There were lights on across the first floor, but no one left the house or came to a door or window.

Within ten minutes of the lights coming on, a car pulled off Sacajawea and up the drive. The motion lamps at the back of the house came on when a late-model minivan pulled into a parking space and cut its lights.

The outside lights coming on just before the visitor's arrival told Levon the car was expected, and the way the driver had pulled into a spot with practiced ease told him this guy was a regular. A man in a shearling coat and a knitted cap exited the car and tromped toward the steps that led to the Dutch door. Before he reached the landing deck, a woman opened it to greet him—a morbidly obese white woman wearing a flower-print apron over a pullover and sweatpants. He focused the binoculars and was able to see that she wore her hair, which framed a heavy cheeked face, in a bowl cut to her shoulders. She was smiling at the newcomer, an expression of welcome. There was a white smudge across her nose. She'd been baking.

In the next twenty minutes, two more vehicles arrived to take up spaces at the back of the house. A pickup truck with a camper top in the bed and a Japanese or Korean import Levon was not familiar with. Two men exited the pickup and were greeted at the back by the woman, who he assumed was Patricia Susanne Dutton. One of them had a brightly wrapped package under one arm. The import was driven by a single man in a black raincoat with a toque with the stripes of some school's colors pulled down over his ears. When their hostess answered the door this time, the apron was gone, and she wore a garish red sweater decorated with snowflakes.

It looked like a normal holiday party, folks getting together to celebrate the season. Lights came on behind two of the barred windows on the second floor. Levon focused on each window but could see nothing, not even projected shadows, through what must have been heavy drapes.

Levon considered taking the house while there were clients inside but rejected the idea, deciding instead to stay with his initial plan of entering the house the following night. That would be New Year's Eve. He considered it to be his best option. He anticipated that there would be few or no visitors. Even men who might visit this house on a regular basis would have obligations to family or friends on a holiday. Far better to take the targets on with the place less occupied. The fewer adults inside, the less chance of things going wrong.

He was only asleep for a few hours when a long freight highballed along the track fifty feet from his hide. The sudden thunder startled him awake, and he struck his head on the roof of the cab. The rumble of the heavy wheels shook the truck, which swayed on its tires in the wind created by their passage. He was slick with sweat, and his breath came in shallow gasps. Levon forced himself to sip air to fill his lungs and let it out easy, then wiped his face dry on a t-shirt and stepped out into the bracing cold.

The red house was dark now, only twenty minutes past midnight. The cars were gone from the back lot.

This was how it would look when he crossed the tracks the next night.

———

THE JUDDER of his cell phone awakened him with an insistent tremble against his hip. He blinked awake. The sun was well up over the horizon. He'd stayed awake for a while after the train had passed. Just before dawn, he'd fallen into a deep, dreamless sleep. Now it was past ten.

He pulled the phone out of his jeans pocket. The screen read Merryberry. He forced an easy tone into his voice and answered it.

"Hey, honey."

"Are you coming home, Daddy?"

It was Hope. His heart swelled a bit to hear her call him Daddy.

"I don't think I'll make it today. I have a few things to do. For sure, I'll be home tomorrow."

"We're going over to Mrs. Hamer's tonight. She invited us there for the new year. Uncle Fern is going with us."

"Well, that sounds like fun."

"More fun if you were here."

"I know, darling. I wish I could be there."

"Yes. I understand." Her voice went low, and there was a shuffling noise.

Merry came on.

"You know Jessie was expecting you to come with us."

"So, you put Hopey on, thinking I'd cave."

"Well, are you?"

"I wish I could. I have some business to see to."

"*That* kind of business?" A tinge of bitterness there now.

"The kind you're better off not knowing about."

"I'm sorry, Daddy." The edge disappeared from Merry's voice.

"Look, you girls have a good time, and if your uncle has too much to drink—"

"I know. I know. Take his truck keys from him and make him stay the night at Jessie's."

"That's my girl. You have fun, okay?"

"Happy New Year, Daddy."

"You too, sweetheart. See you tomorrow."

The line went dead on Merry's end.

45

Levon saw no reason to risk staying in place all day and being seen along the tracks. He drove the Avalanche back down the township road and then the county road and an hour west to the next town over. It was a college town, and though it was dead over the holidays with the students gone on break, it showed more signs of life than Brillings. He had breakfast at a Huddle House, served by a waitress too drowsy or hungover to ever remember him.

He killed some time by walking a path around a local reservoir. He saw a few joggers there but was mostly alone for the ten-mile walk around the icy expanse. The cold air calmed him, and he listened to the wind off the water rustling the tops of the trees in a susurrating whisper. He'd taken long walks like this with Arlene before and after Merry came along. Somehow, despite having parents whose idea of camping was staying at an Embassy Suites instead of a Four Seasons, Arlene had been an outdoors lover. Levon had spent more of his life under the sky than indoors, and to him, the deep woods or an endless field of grass was like coming home.

He missed their walks. He missed her smile. He missed the talks and the silences. He'd even have given anything to have her back for one of their infrequent but impassioned arguments. From their very first meeting, Levon had always been easy around Arlene. With her, he could pack the past away and just enjoy her company. With her, tomorrow didn't matter either.

If he'd only had more time. A few more years. All those deployments away with her alone. He'd never get them back, never be able to make it up to her.

Whatever happened tonight, he'd drop this hunt. It ended at the red house no matter which way it fell. He'd drive back to the holler tomorrow and never leave again. He owed Merry that. Hope, too. Most of all, he owed it to Arlene.

He picked up some burgers at a drive-through on the way back to Brillings. He'd eat them when he arrived and catch a few more hours' sleep in the truck before crossing the tracks.

An Ace Hardware anchored a strip mall on the way out of town. He pulled into the lot just before closing and bought a few items from a clearance rack at the front of the store. The two young girls at the counter were too busy talking about their plans for the evening to pay him any mind.

————

THE LOWERING skies opened to release a mix of rain and sleet that turned to ice on every surface. The branches of the trees turned crystalline, creating a glittering display in the Avalanche's headlight beams. Dusk came early; a dreary gloom settled from horizon to horizon on both sides of the township road.

He cut his lights when he turned onto the service

road and followed the tracks back to his hide, then reversed into the sumacs where he'd parked before. He climbed into the bed to survey the red house using his night-vision monocular. The reach wasn't the same, and the NODs tech blurred the image. It was clear enough that he could see the welcome lights were on at the front and side of the house. There were also a half-dozen cars in the rear parking area. He watched another arrival. A figure in a hooded coat hurried, shoulders hunched against the rain, to the back door and was caught in the yellow glow of the doorway for a moment.

His assumptions had been wrong. Instead of this evening being a dead night, the Duttons appeared to be throwing a party. As the sky grew darker, he watched the house. More headlights came up the driveway until the rear yard was at capacity, with eleven cars parked on the gravel. That added up to at least thirteen targets inside, maybe more.

He could come back another night, only he'd made a promise to himself and to Merry and an unspoken one to Arlene. However this ended, it ended tonight.

It was getting close to ten o'clock, and no more cars had arrived. The guests were settled in, the party in full swing. No one would be leaving before midnight.

At 11:15, he drove the Avalanche off the service road to circle back to the red house on Sacajawea. He turned left through the gap in the wall and drove to the house, headlights on as if he were a late-arriving guest. Just past the front of the house, he braked the truck and killed the engine. He slipped the car keys into his jeans pocket and opened the rear door, where he pulled out a long box wrapped in the Christmas tree-themed paper and red ribbon he'd bought at the Ace. His customary .45 and two spare magazines were snugged into the holster at the small of his back alongside a dagger in a sheath.

He pulled aside the rear seatback to take out a second .45, which he secured in his waistband behind his belt buckle. He snagged a hammerless .38 revolver from a peg on the rear wall of the cab and dropped it into the pocket of his barn coat, which he then buttoned closed. Before stepping out of the truck, he took a pair of clamp pliers from a red Ace bag and put them in the coat pocket opposite the snubby.

Ball cap pulled low on his forehead, he walked down the gravel drive to the front of the house. There was music coming from inside. The song had a heavy beat, but only the resonance of it could be heard through the glass of the windows running down the side of the house. The pulsing blue glare of a television could be seen against the curtains. He followed the walkway to a broad set of steps leading to the porch. A creaking sound made him turn as he crossed to the door.

"That a gift for Trish or the kids?"

Levon turned to where a figure sat in a high-backed wicker chair, the weight of the man causing the chair to complain. The glow of a lighter gave the heavy-set man's face a ghostly appearance in the gloom.

"A train set. For the kids," Levon answered. The box had once held the miniature train set he'd bought at the hardware store. The tracks and engine and cars were now in a trash bag in the bed of the Avalanche.

"I used to love trains when I was little," the man said and took a drag on a cigar, the end of it a red coal in the shadows gathered at the corner of the porch.

"What boy doesn't like a railroad set?" Levon stepped closer to the seated man, voice easy.

"Didn't bring anything for the girls?" the man asked, a teasing tone in his voice.

"I wasn't sure there'd be girls." Levon moved closer as

though he were about to take a seat in the chair next to the man. "I haven't been here in a while."

The man chuckled, releasing a cloud of smoke that wreathed his face. "What's a party without girls, right?"

"How many? Girls, I mean?"

"Three. No, four. And six boys. Some new flesh here tonight. You know, I don't think we've met be—"

The man's question was interrupted by the spade-shaped blade of a dagger thrust up through the soft flesh just under his chin. The six-inch blade rammed through his palate into his brain. Levon held a fistful of the man's hair and gave the blade a sharp twist to the left and right before pulling it free. He wiped it clean on the front of the man's woolen coat before restoring it to the sheath on his belt. He removed the cigar from the man's dead fingers and smeared it cold in the dampness atop a porch railing.

It was open house, so he pulled back the storm door, then the solid-core front door and went inside. He found himself in an enclosed entryway. The walls were hung with winter coats, and some galoshes stood in puddles on the stone floor. The room smelled like a wet dog. He closed the door and found it had been fitted with two deadbolts set above and below the knob. He used the keys in the locks to throw the bolts, then put both keys in the watch pocket of his jeans. He stepped to the interior door, a heavy affair of white wood with a beveled glass center, upon which hung a wreath of holly dotted with pinecones frosted in faux snow.

The house was warm and had a fug of smoke in the air, tobacco mixed with marijuana. There were two men standing by the fireplace in the broad living room. Levon's arrival interrupted their conversation, and they turned to him with expectant smiles.

"That for the kids?" one of them asked.

"Train set," Levon said.

"Cool," the other said, eyes red-rimmed from the stub of a joint held between his fingers.

"Put it over there, I guess." The first one waggled a finger at the Christmas tree in one corner of the room. There were other wrapped presents there, as well as opened toys.

"We're gonna have the kids down after midnight to open 'em," the toker said.

The other one sniggered.

Levon rested the package against a wall by the tree.

"Guess I'd better go in and make my hellos," he said and made his way to a hall next to a staircase that led to the dark second floor. He removed his leather gloves. Underneath, he wore flesh-colored vinyl gloves.

Both sides of the hall were lined with framed photographs: old family portraits, faded shots of a young man posing in a football uniform, graduation and wedding pictures, two photos of the same Labrador retriever, one of the dog sleeping on a sofa and the other of him holding a ball in his mouth on a lawn. The pictures of the dog were old, turned bluish with time. That didn't mean they didn't currently have a dog, though he hadn't seen one in the yard the entire time he'd watched the house.

The hall opened into what was meant to be a formal dining room, now a party room with a wall-mounted big-screen TV with the sound turned up—some musical celebration of the coming new year with a countdown clock in the corner of the screen. The large room ran the full width of the house. Levon counted six guests standing in groups or helping themselves to cold cuts and bowls of salads set on a table against one wall. Most of them held beers or drink tumblers. Only a couple of the men checked out the new arrival before turning back to their conversations.

The large woman Levon had seen acting as greeter the evening before entered from the brightly lit kitchen at the back of the house. She held a tray of cookies in oven-mittened hands, her hip pushing the swinging door wide. She wore an apron with a candy cane print.

"Cookies and beer, Trish?" someone said from near the snack table.

"They're for the kids, stupid," the woman said with a smile. She removed cookies from the tray with care to place them in a bowl fashioned like a snowman's head. It was already half-filled with the same kind of cookies, cut in the shapes of pine trees and stars.

Her back was turned to the kitchen door, and Levon stepped behind her to push his way through the swinging door into the kitchen. A man was at the open freezer door scooping ice cubes from a bin into a bucket. It was a white-tiled kitchen with old steel fixtures painted sky blue and topped with speckled red Formica. He scanned the daisy-yellow linoleum floor and saw no food or water bowls for a dog.

"They gonna need more rolls out there or—" The man turned, eyebrows raised.

"Happy New Year," Levon said, crossing the room toward the man, his hand out.

"I don't know you," Ed Dutton said.

Levon drove the heel of his hand into Ed's forehead, hurling the back of his skull into the top of the open freezer's frame. Stunned, the man offered no resistance when the bucket and scoop fell to the floor, sending ice scattering over the tiles. Levon got him in a chokehold and searched the room until his eyes fell on the open doorway of the pantry.

The heels of Ed's shoes squeaked on the linoleum as Levon dragged him backward into the pantry. The man enclosed in Levon's arm fought feebly. His carotid and jugular crushed flat, his brain was soon starved of oxygen, and he sagged to the floor. Levon dropped him to the linoleum and leapt to draw the pantry door closed. He plucked a dishtowel from atop a folded stack and shoved it into the man's mouth, then secured a zip-tie around the man's wrists and another about his ankles.

"Ed?"

The woman's voice came through the pantry door. Levon crouched.

"Ed, dammit! There's ice *everywhere*!"

Levon watched a shadow cross the gap at the bottom of the pantry door.

"Well, *I'm* not cleaning it up, you fucker!"

He heard her heavy tread across the room and the squeak and clap of the swinging door. The kitchen was empty again.

He passed through the kitchen into the mud room at the back of the house. Here he found the Dutch door he'd seen from the outside. It was secured with a single deadbolt, the key still in the lock. Using the clamp pliers, he got a grip on the key's head and bent it back and forth until it snapped off, leaving the shaft jammed in the slot.

He exited the kitchen through the swinging doors to find Trish bitching to some of the guests about what a goddamned slob her husband was and asking if anyone had seen him. Someone suggested maybe he was opening his present early. That was answered with more remarks and suppressed laughter.

Moving easily, Levon made his way to the house's central hall, where he found the two guys he'd met upon entering the house. They were bent over an open package by the tree. They had the wrapping and ribbon off and had opened the box of the Disney Railroad Electric Train Set, only to find it contained a 12-gauge Saiga semi-auto shotgun.

46

He brought the men down with center shots from the .45. They crashed into the tree, which toppled with the clatter and clash of falling ornaments. Shouts rose from the back of the house.

Levon turned to the hall in time to see a man, face drained of blood and eyes like glass, sliding to a halt on the floorboards, arms out to restore his balance. A double-tap to the chest sent the man to the floor. Two more rounds fired down the hall discouraged anyone else who might be curious.

Snatching up the Saiga, Levon stepped toward the fireplace, out of sight of the hallway. He fired his last two .45 rounds into the still-moving bodies under the tree before slipping a fresh magazine into the spent .45, then replaced the handgun in his waistband, the heat of the barrel radiating through his shirttail. The dining room went dark except for the fluttering light from the television. The loud voices had died to a hush. There were raised voices from further back, in the kitchen.

He pulled back the bolt to charge the shotgun with the first round from a pair of ten-round magazines and stepped from cover to send a load of buck toward the back of the house. The heavy load caught a man who was sliding along the wall of the hall full in the face and upper body. He slumped by the other guy Levon had dropped in the hallway. An automatic pistol fell out of the man's grip.

A flash of light from the now-dark dining room. Behind Levon, a bullet punched a hole in the living room wall with a flat slap. Levon aimed a three-round burst at the source of the flash, and the broad spray of double-ought peppered the walls around the dining room archway. A high, keening squeal rose out of the darkness. Levon moved as he fired, gaining the foot of the staircase. He was once more out of the line of sight from the dining room. The music from the other room went dead.

Movement from above him caused him to duck while swinging the shotgun barrel upward. Bullets raised a cloud of plaster dust from the wall behind him. A shower of glass from a shattered picture frame glittered on the stair carpet like diamonds.

A load of buck took the man descending the stairs in both legs. He tumbled toward Levon, a stubby black cut-down AK-47 falling from his hands. Levon picked up the rifle and pumped rounds into the bleeding mewling figure at his feet until it was silent. He emptied the AK's magazine down the hall before tossing it aside.

He scanned the darkness above. He didn't know if the man who'd come from the second floor had been up there when he arrived. If not, it meant there was another stairway somewhere in the house. Not for the first time, he regretted not having seen a floorplan.

"You out there!" a voice called from the darkness. It was the lady of the house.

Levon put his back to the staircase wall where he

could see up the steps and through the banisters to the hall.

"We're calling the police!" she shouted.

Bullshit. You say you *called* the police, not you're *calling* them. She was using the police as a threat. She had no intention of calling them. That didn't mean there wasn't *some* kind of help she could call in. Levon was on a timetable now. He could hear their muted conversation in the other room. He switched out mags on the shotgun for a full load of ten with one in the chamber.

"Is it money?" she called again. "Is that what you want?"

He stepped into the clear, the Saiga at his hip, and fired a four-round barrage that ended in two rifled slugs that punched dinner-plate-sized holes through the plaster walls. Screams erupted from the dining room, cutting through the buzz left by the booms of the shotgun. Levon entered the dining room at a walk. Four men lay on the floor in a mess of plaster dust and glass. A fifth was crawling near the overturned snack table, hands and knees slipping in spilled potato salad. He had a revolver clutched in one fist. A pumpkin ball sent him crashing into a settee in a burst of blood and bone.

A load of buck removed the swinging door from its frame. The bright light from the kitchen threw a bar of illumination across the dining room. Shots came from the back, someone firing wild and blind. A round exploded the cookie bowl, making a pinata of Frosty's head.

Levon backed away at an angle, emptying the remaining rounds through the shared wall between the rooms. Light streamed through the ragged holes. A series of loud, wet gasps came from the kitchen. No more shots were fired.

He leaned the shotgun against a chair arm and pulled

out both .45s. Moving low, he approached the open doorway, staying outside the rectangle of light it cast on the littered floor. He listened to the sounds from the other room, whimpering punctuated by an ugly rasping cough. Whispered voices. Curses. Hard to tell the gender.

With a leap, he crossed the bar of light to the other side of the door. No one took a shot, so he lunged through the kitchen door, the Colts raised in his hands. A man lay sprawled on the floor in a pool of blood, eyes scared and crimson bubbles on his lips. In the mudroom, another man was clawing at the back door, trying to work the locks open.

Trish Dutton reacted with a shriek, a mad ululating howl of rage. She rushed across the floor, a cleaver held high in one chubby fist.

A slug took her through the forehead, and she stumbled back across the room until she crashed into the front of the range to land on her rear on the linoleum. Levon put two more through her chest before turning to the man now calling for Jesus to help him get the goddamned back door open. Blood ran down the door; he'd slashed his fingers on the jagged edge of the broken deadbolt key.

Levon triple-tapped him through the back before putting the handguns on a counter to cool.

He went to the sink and washed the blood spatter from his gloved hands. With a damp dishtowel, he wiped the blood from his face and neck. He put the towel in his coat pocket. He'd burn that and his clothes somewhere between here and home.

Ed Dutton lay on the pantry floor in a puddle of his own piss. His eyes were wide and red-rimmed, streaming with tears. Strings of snot ran from his nose with each wheezing breath.

Levon crouched and pulled the gag out of his mouth. Ed let out a wordless, wailing cry that faded to a gibbering sob. Levon took a gallon jug of vinegar from a shelf and poured it over Ed's face until the man was sputtering and coughing.

"Do you know this man?" Levon held his smartphone up to Ed's wavering eyes.

"Who are you?" Ed could only manage a croak.

"It's too late for that, Ed. Do you know this man?"

"El Capitan," Ed said, fresh tears welling in his eyes.

"The only way out of this for you is to tell me his real name."

Ed told Levon the name. Levon stood, removing the .38 from his coat pocket.

"You told me if I gave you the name, it was my way out." Ed was convulsing, fighting to free his hands and feet in a final feral struggle.

"This was always your only way out." Levon stepped back to avoid the blood spray.

47

The locks on the rooms upstairs were opened by a master key on a chain with some kind of rubber cartoon character on it—a yellow cat with tiny legs and long ears. The back half of the house was lined with evenly spaced doorways with matching deadbolt locks and peepholes. This was not the original design of the house, but a customization. Where there should have been perhaps four bedrooms and a bath, there were more than a dozen smaller rooms with doorways set no more than two feet apart.

Levon knocked before putting the key in the lock of the first door.

"It's all right now. Nothing to be scared of."

There was no answer from inside, and he keyed the lock to enter.

The room was a windowless cell with a cot against one wall and a scarred dresser against the other. There was a plastic Lowes bucket in a corner for a toilet. In the light from the hallway, Levon could see, seated on the edge of the bed, a child in pajamas regarding him with shining eyes.

"You want to come on out here, son?"

The boy looked at Levon warily. His eyes were pale in the scant light, deep circles under them. The eyes were much older than this boy's age. Levon guessed he was around seven.

"Your choice. Nobody's going to make you, all right?"

The boy looked past Levon, studying the empty hallway behind him.

"Look, you come out in your own good time. I'm going to be leaving now. You'll never see me again. In fact, it'll be like I was never here."

The boy returned his gaze to Levon's face.

"I'm putting these on the floor for you right here." Levon set the keyring with the yellow cat on the carpet just outside the door. Next to it, he placed a burner phone he'd bought for this purpose. It was pre-paid off a card, bought with cash months before up in Tennessee.

The boy looked at the key and phone.

"You use that key, and you open the other doors here. You let the kids out, okay?"

The boy goggled.

"Do you hear me, son?"

The boy nodded.

"Then you use this phone. You dial nine-one-one, and you talk to the police. Can you read?"

The boy nodded again, this time more emphatically.

"You tell them this is where you are." Levon laid an envelope on the floor by the keys and phone. It was an unopened electric bill he'd found in a basket atop the refrigerator that bore the address of the house. "And you stay on the phone with whoever answers until you know the police are here. You understand?"

"Yes," the boy said in a clear voice.

"You and the other kids stay up here until the police get here. All right? Don't go downstairs. Stay on the phone and stay up here, and the police will come to take you away from here."

"Where will they take us?" the boy asked, a quaver in his voice.

"That I don't know. But you're never coming back here, and you'll never see the people who live here ever again. You understand what I said to you? You're all right to do all the things I asked you to do?"

"Yes."

"Good. That's real good. You stay strong and help the others. I've got to go now."

"Mister?"

"What is it, son?"

"Are they dead?" the boy asked, voice strong again.

"They're all dead. Every one of them."

"Thank you," the boy said, his eyes brimming.

48

Uncle Fern did have a few too many while ringing in the new year.

They all slept in the next morning after talking late into the night. Jessie made a bed for the Cade girls on a sleeper sofa in her family room. Fern crapped out on the living room sofa, and she made sure he was covered with a comforter and blanket as the fire died in the ceramic stove.

In the morning—closer to noon, really—Jessie went to wake her daughter to help her make breakfast for everyone. Sandy moaned and waved a feeble hand before burying her head in the pillow.

Jessie soldiered on into the kitchen and started the coffee before getting out the ingredients for pancakes. She set frozen strawberries in a colander under the cold water tap to thaw while she assembled the batter in the big yellow mixing bowl that had been her mom's. She got the griddle going and returned to her daughter's room to shake Sandy awake.

"You're making pancakes with strawberries," she said in her sternest parental tone. "I have to see to the barn."

Sandy's answer was an extended, "Mooooooooooom," but she was upright and poking her feet into slippers.

"Just pour the batter and keep an eye on it." Jessie pulled on a fleece-lined barn coat hanging from a hook by the back door. "And don't go back to bed!"

"Coffee," Sandy said with a low groan as she stumbled into the kitchen, hands held before her in zombie fashion.

In the barn, Jessie opened the doors to the paddock and distributed flakes of hay on the ground before unlatching the stall doors to let the ponies outside. She was in the middle of forking clumps of manure out of the straw bed of the second stall when she heard the dogs bark.

The Cades had brought their animals with them. Part of the family. The bluetick was howling in the barnyard while the yapping bark of the pesky terrier was fading in the distance as he took off somewhere.

She stepped outside to see a truck coming up the drive, the Jack Russell racing to meet it.

The Avalanche pulled to a stop on the gravel in front of the barn. She stepped closer, and before she could say a word, Levon was out of the cab and had her in his arms.

"This is different," she said against his ear.

"I damn sure hope so," he replied, his hold tightening.

"You're thinking of making a permanent change?"

"Shut up," he said, but she could hear the smile in his voice.

They kissed, only interrupted by Rascal's paws on their legs. Levon kicked out at the dog. He turned to scamper off in a spray of gravel.

"So, this is the new you?" she asked when they'd broken their embrace. They kept a grip on each other's arms.

"I don't know about that." He looked away. "Same old me. Just have to find a new way forward."

"I know it's hard, Levon. Hard to put all that shit behind you. But can you at least try and make peace with it?"

"Yeah." He looked at her. "I'm gonna try. For my girls. For Fernie. The business, you know."

"Hell of a thing when being a moonshiner is a step *up* for a mountain boy."

"That's the sad truth of it, huh?"

"And what about us?" She searched his eyes.

His grip tightened on her arms through the heavy cloth of the barn coat. He was about to say something when a shout from the house broke the silence.

Merry and Hope exploded outside in a race for the Avalanche. Levon dropped to a knee, arms outspread as the girls crashed into him. He gathered them in an embrace and held them.

Held them like he'd never let them go.

A LOOK AT: LEVON'S PREY
LEVON CADE BOOK 10

Book ten in the dark and action-packed vigilante justice thriller series—Levon Cade.

Levon Cade stirred up a hornet's nest when he uncovered a child trafficking ring—earning the attention of a congressman and a major player in the conspiracy who's made it his mission to find Levon at all costs.

At the same time, Levon's Uncle Fern, a former moonshiner, is starting up a legitimate distillery business, bringing him into conflict with a moonshining clan and past rival of the Cades.

Both proving mounting distractions, Levon is caught by surprise when a private investigator—whose sole purpose is to end the threat that Levon embodies—finds him and vows to gun him and his family down.

All Levon wants is to be left alone to raise his daughters in peace...but these enemies are begging to be put to sleep.

Grab your copy now and join Levon as he faces his most formidable adversaries yet, all while striving to safeguard his family and maintain the tranquility he so desperately craves.

AVAILABLE NOW

vision series from Silvester Sistance, Ballou Production. He currently lives in central Florida and he
does not miss the snow.

ABOUT THE AUTHOR

Born and raised in Philadelphia, Chuck Dixon worked a
variety of jobs from driving an ice cream truck to
working graveyard at a 7-11 before trying his hand as a
writer. After a brief sojourn in children's books he
turned to his childhood love of comic books. In his
thirty years as a writer for Marvel, DC Comics and other
publishers, Chuck built a reputation as a prolific and
versatile freelancer working on a wide variety titles and
genres from Conan the Barbarian to SpongeBob Square-
Pants. His graphic novel adaptation of J.R.R.
Tolkien's *The Hobbit* continues to be an international
bestseller translated into fifty languages. He is the co-
creator (with Graham Nolan) of the Batman villain Bane,
the first enduring member added to the Dark Knight's
rogue's gallery in forty years. He was also one of the
seminal writers responsible for the continuing popu-
larity of Marvel Comics' The Punisher.

After making his name in comics, Chuck moved to
prose in 2011 and has since written over twenty novels,
mostly in the action-thriller genre with a few side-trips
to horror, hardboiled noir and western. The transition
from the comics form to prose has been a life-altering
event for him. As Chuck says, *"writing a comic is like
getting on a roller coaster while writing a novel is more like a
long car trip with a bunch of people you'll learn to hate."* His
Levon Cade novels are currently in production as a tele-

vision series from Sylvester Stallone's Balboa Productions. He currently lives in central Florida and, no, he does not miss the snow.